# ENGINE OF MY DREAMS

## GLENN ERIC

### BEACHFRONT ENTERTAINMENT

# ENGINE OF MY DREAMS

1991

# 1

"How can you say you're getting older, when you don't believe in time?" blurted a voice from out of nowhere.

"Excuse me?" Michael froze in his tracks, his brow wrinkling as naturally as yesterday's bedsheets.

"Sure the sun's getting colder, but how can you say that it's dying?"

Michael paused, gazing down at Kenji Murakami, the gaunt and oddly long-legged though short-statured, Japanese-born, cultural anthropologist. Murakami was a normally reserved and aloof fellow who rarely spoke to his colleagues unnecessarily. Unless it was about baseball statistics. He was a fanatic for baseball statistics. This seemed to have nothing to do with baseball so far as Michael could tell. This was one of those exceptional moments. He was caught off guard.

And what was Kenji going on about? *How can you say you're getting older, when you don't believe in time?*

"What do you mean?"

"Deep, eh?" Kenji said. Without waiting for Michael's reply, he added, "It's poetry."

"Oh, right. Poetry." Michael waited, expecting something more. *Was* there something more coming? Words of Kenji enlightenment?

"I thought you might like it," said Murakami. He handed the book over. It was slender and bound in heavy red leather that stuck to Michael's fingers. He slowly opened the cover and ran his fingers over the contents. The pages were thick as wax paper and rough to the touch. "Thanks."

"Quite. Please, let me know what you think." Feet shuffled off.

"Yes," Michael called after the echoing shoes. He stopped at the threshold to his office and struggled with his keys, all the while thinking what an odd lot cultural anthropologists were.

The somewhat tarnished brass sign on the door read *Aaron Michael Hart*. There were no initials suggesting his pedigree as most his colleagues had appended to their nameplates, Ph.D., Esq., etc. He had no need for such things.

Michael opened the door and stepped inside.

His office was small and windowless. Michael might as well have been cruising one thousand fathoms under the cold Antarctic Circle, cutting through the frigid waters of the Amundsen Sea in a nuclear submarine.

Come to think of it, sometimes Michael felt as if his whole life so far could have been described that way. Cruising along at fifteen knots with a thousand fathoms of water over his head and miles of ocean around him; between himself and the rest of humanity.

It was funny to think that just such a man had become an anthropologist, a studier of Man.

Or maybe it was apropos.

Perhaps being an outsider, and a stubborn loner, made it easier for Michael (no one called him Aaron but his mother) to understand his subject. Though, in fact, his subject was long since dead. He was an anthropologist but his specialty was archaeology. Even the children and trinkets that he studied were at least a thousand years old.

Michael left the office door open and turned on the desk lamp. He glanced at the ancient clock radio on the bookshelf across the narrow room. Its face was yellowed and cracking from the strain of keeping up with time all these countless years.

It was nearly noon and his next class was a twelve-thirty, pre-Columbian art history survey.

Michael gathered together his slides and skimmed through a recent tome on pre-Columbian man in Costa Rica. The slides comprised a collection of photographs which Michael had shot over the pre-grad school years, depicting public art and artifacts in the culturally-rich Mesoamerican region.

Students often chided him for not using a computer and one or two had even offered to transfer all his slides to a computer program. He'd politely declined the offers. Something about handling those slides, feeling their sharp paper edges on his fingers, felt right.

He knew he'd have to enter the modern world one day, but was in no hurry to become 'digitalized' as he feared all of mankind was in danger of becoming. Machines and big business, they absorbed everything in their paths, including people, including history.

His eyes flicked across the glossy pages of his book. He rubbed his temples. He shook his head. It was going to be hard staying awake until class time.

The telephone on his desk rang out loudly, jolting him from his deteriorating consciousness. He answered it on the first chirruping ring. "Hello?" he said softly.

Michael had always spoken softly, almost timidly. As if he feared that if he spoke too loudly, too fiercely, he would wake the world, maybe even the dead, if they were listening.

"Hello, Son," said Taft Hart, Michael's father.

"Hi, Dad," said Michael with surprise and yet very little emotion. "How are you? Is everything all right?"

"Sure, sure. No problems," said Taft. He scratched his chin. Nervous. "I just wanted to check on you. You still coming next week?"

"Of course," answered Michael. "I've got the ticket right here in my desk somewhere." He opened the pencil drawer and pushed aside napkins, potsherds, pens and loose change in a vain attempt at finding his airline tickets. He knew they were in there somewhere.

"Okay, well..." replied Mr. Hart, rather uncomfortably. Taft Hart owed his name to his own father who had decided to bless or curse his son with the first name of Taft. He was, of course, namesaked to William Howard Taft, twenty-seventh President of the United States and tenth Chief Justice of the Supreme Court (and no, the Supreme Court was not the name of Diana Ross's old backup group—they were simply Supremes—though surely any of the esteemed jurists would have died for a chance to sing Motown doo-wahs behind the legendary chanteuse rather than sit around in their heavy robes in their dreary chambers reading law journals).

Taft Hart's father, Nathaniel, had been one of the twenty-seventh president's most ardent fans. "Any man who holds public office and says 'politics makes him sick' has got my vote," Nathaniel was often heard to say.

Taft in itself was not such a bad name.

Unfortunately, when one compounded that name with the family name of Hart there was bound to be confusion. Whenever Taft Hart introduced himself to a group of people there was always one in the party who said "Gee, that name sounds familiar. Don't I know you?"

Of course, they did not. It was just that Taft Hart sounded awfully like Taft-Hartley and most every school attending half-awake child in Social Studies had at least heard of the Taft-Hartley Act; whether they thought it was an old burlesque team or two girls named 'Ginger' who did perverse things to one another in blue movies or, worse yet, some boring detail of American civics that was best left unexplored.

The one and only time Taft had complained of his name to his father was the year nineteen forty-seven when the Taft-Hartley Law was promulgated. Taft Hart was himself twenty-seven years old at that time and no child himself. "Whatcha gonna do?" said Nathaniel, better known as Nate. "Change your name?"

Taft answered no.

"You know," said Nate, with some profundity (it was left over from that morning's checker game held in the front window of the Irish grocer's on Lafayette Street), "I was going to name you Sears Roebuck Hart. It's a strong name and it was my first choice. I figured you could always get a job with the company then, too.

"After all, how could they refuse to hire a Mister Sears Roebuck Hart? It'd be bad karma for them, real bad," he said drawing out his words.

"Of course, your mother threatened to withhold relations if I did," enlightened Nathaniel.

What a coincidence that the former president's son, Senator Robert Taft should team up with a member of the House of Representatives named Fred Allan (did his father not mind the unavoidable references to the radio comedian?) Hartley?

This was a coincidence Taft Hart could easily have lived without. Because ever since nineteen hundred and forty-seven he had been answering the inevitable question, "Don't I know you from somewhere?" He then would have to explain the machinations of Nate Hart's mind, William Taft's term of presidency, the quirk of having a law on the books concerning the Labor-Relations Management Act and his own non-role in the twisted affair.

In fact, Taft Hart was quite certain that more people were made aware of the Taft-Hartley Act through him than had ever read about it, let alone remembered it from their high school civics books. (Not to mention, most kids these days think Civic's just a Japanese automobile.) Taft had, by twist of fate, become something of an educator and you could spell that with a capital E.

"Dad?"

"Huh, what?"

"You didn't answer me. Is everything all right?" repeated Michael.

"Sure, sure," said Taft. "What was it you asked me? Guess my hearing's starting to go," he clucked.

"I asked how Mother was doing—"

"Oh, yeah. Right, right," said Taft, guardedly. Taft Hart had a habit of compounding words. Duplicating them with neither rhyme nor reason nor rules, at least not that anyone in the immediate family had been able to decode. For years it was a joke in the family to call him Dad Dad.

"How you doing, Dad Dad?"

"Fine, fine," he'd say, without once catching on to the joke. Elizabeth, the eldest of his daughters still called him Dad Dad.

"Mother's fine, just fine."

"Put her on the phone, will you?" requested Michael. "I've got a few minutes before class," he said, stealing a look at the dusty clock that now showed twelve-seventeen. The dust had, quietly and uninvited, settled into the office about the same time Michael did.

"Sorry, Michael," said Taft. "She's gone out shopping. You know how women are." He chuckled for Michael's benefit.

"Oh," said Michael with unmasked disappointment. "Tell her I said hello."

"Of course I will, of course I will," Taft agreed. "Well, gotta go, kiddo. This is long distance, you know. I only wanted to make sure you were still flying flying out."

"Yes, Dad. I'll be there next week."

"Okay, Son. We'll see you then. Don't worry about a car, I'll pick you up at the airport."

"Thanks, but you'd better call the airline first and make sure the flight's going to be on time, Dad."

"Sure, sure," answered Taft. "Well," he said after some pause, "see you next week. Look forward to having you."

"Me too, Dad. Bye." Michael hung up the telephone. On the other end of the line, Taft did the same. Michael looked forward to his sojourn home. Taft, on the other hand, was dreading it.

"Doctor, I mean, Michael?"

Michael looked up toward the door. Rebecca stood peeking in past the rim. "Yes, Rebecca?"

"I wanted to let you know that it's time for your class."

"Oh, thanks." Michael stood. The secretary lingered in the doorway. "Is there anything else?"

"No," she said with hesitation. "I guess not." She had been hoping to strike up some sort of conversation with the young professor but had no idea how to go about it. He seemed so unapproachable, as if he'd launched himself off in his own little skiff and kept all others at bay.

Maybe he didn't find her type attractive?

Still, she knew without being egotistical about it that many men did. In fact, she could be considered quite beautiful in a quiet sort of way, so she'd been told. She was only twenty-six years old, yet she'd had her share of boyfriends and admirers. None that she'd been entirely satisfied with. Maybe Professor Hart didn't like brunettes?

She wondered what type he did like. Rebecca had only been on the job for a little over two months and hadn't seen Michael acting in anything more than a professional manner with any of the many women he came into contact with on campus. There were plenty, too. The University of California at Santa Barbara was not, after all, a monastery.

She said goodbye to Michael as he packed his boxes of slides under one arm and gripped his briefcase in his free hand. He turned the corner and disappeared from view.

She found him very attractive, if perhaps too brooding. Michael's blue eyes changed color with his moods. Fine blond hair fell naturally back from his face. He kept his hair cut quite short and this only served to highlight his strong facial features. Definitely flattering, she thought, yet he probably didn't even realize it.

Rebecca couldn't imagine Michael giving any attention to his person in terms of trying to please or be attractive to others. With him, it seemed wholly natural, unintentional even. Generally, he wore loose shirts and nondescript trousers with dark leather shoes.

Michael was just under six foot tall and had an athlete's natural abilities though he had never applied himself in that area of life.

Rebecca, turning, deep in thought, bumped into Professor Bandry in the hallway. "Sorry," she blurted, red-faced and apologetic.

"That's all right, Rebecca," answered the genial Professor of Social Anthropology.

Rebecca liked the gentle social anthropologist well enough, albeit he came across as somewhat pompous (he reminded her of a domesticated and well-fed brown bear). Perhaps it was the Harvard accent which made him sound so snooty. It was especially odd coming from a man who'd attended the University of Michigan in Ann Arbor. She knew. She'd looked up his personnel file.

"It was my fault," said Professor Bandry. "I saw you standing there apparently lost in thought. I guess I should have stomped my feet or whistled before attempting to pass!"

Rebecca laughed. "You're very funny, Professor." She looked once more at Michael's officer door and sighed. "I'd better get back to my desk."

"I'll follow you," said the professor. "I was just coming to get my mail."

"Let me get it for you," answered Rebecca, leading the way back to her own office. "That's my job, after all."

Her office was in the anterior of a larger office housing the Chairman of the Department of Anthropology. Rebecca served as both department secretary and receptionist.

"Here you are." Rebecca reached into Professor Bandry's box and removed a motley assortment consisting of all sizes and shapes and colors of letters, brochures, book reviews and newsletters that she then placed in his extended hands.

"Thank you, my dear," said Professor Bandry.

He took his leave and Rebecca was left alone in the office. The department chairman, Randall Cane, was out of town attending a conference titled North American Native Linguistic Influences, in Atlanta. She imagined Michael beginning his lecture just as he, indeed, was only opening the door to the classroom.

So she was a little off temporally, it was close.

The lecture was moribund. Michael realized that from the onset. As he gazed around the room, he wondered if the students were thinking so as well. He looked out at the class from his podium. Some lazily pushed their pencils over yellow legal pads.

Others seemed lost in worlds of their own.

Gloomily, he replaced his slides and put together his notes. Taking every trace of himself off the table that served as a desk. Each time he did so, he felt like some sort of primitive inquiline creature always bedding down in someone else's home and never his own.

He fielded the last-minute questions that invariably came up in the form of one or more students crowding around the table and vying for his attention like excitable celebrity seekers.

Afterward, he went back to his office across campus and thought about lunch. It was precisely two o'clock. He thought about lunch but he didn't eat any. He didn't leave his office even though he had no more classes that afternoon.

Michael read his notes for the next day, then made some changes to a thesis he was writing on Pre-Columbian trade in Mesoamerica.

He gave up on work when the battery in his laptop died and he couldn't find the power cord and adapter. Thinking about his pending trip, he phoned his credit union to see where his balance stood at present.

He also conducted a valiant and fruitless last-ditch effort to find his airline tickets. It was no use. He'd lost them. He cursed himself, wondering what the airline's policy would be in this situation. Would they provide new tickets? Would they charge him for them?

He had no telephone directory in his office (a phone book would have taken up valuable space) so he dialed up Rebecca's extension. It was now five o'clock in the afternoon and he wasn't sure if she would be at her desk. She was.

"Hello, Department of Anthropology," answered Rebecca crisply.

"Hello, Rebecca, it's Michael Hart."

She'd recognized his voice instantly. "Hi," she said with sudden keenness. "I'm surprised you're still here. Everyone else has gone home."

Michael didn't know what to say to this. He wasn't good at

small talk and so he skated right around the comment. "I was wondering if you would do me a favor and look up the number of an airline for me?"

"Sure," she said. "Hold on, let me get the phone book." Rebecca set the phone on her blotter and reached for the telephone directory atop the tall metal file cabinet behind her desk. "Okay," she said, "Got it."

She started flipping pages, looking for the airlines section of the yellow pages. "There isn't a problem with your tickets for next week or anything, is there?"

Michael stopped mid-thought, in surprise. He wouldn't have imagined that she'd even known about his upcoming trip, if he'd bothered to think about her at all. "Why, yes, there is," he said, somewhat abashedly. "I'm afraid I've lost them. I don't know what the airline will do now."

"Lost them?"

"Yes," affirmed Michael.

"That's funny."

"What do you mean?"

"Well, you gave me the tickets and asked me to hold them for you. I don't remember giving them back to you." Already, Rebecca was looking in her desk drawer where she'd remembered placing Michael's plane tickets for safe keeping. "Unless you came and got them from my desk when I—no." She pulled aside a package of miniature Kleenex. "Yep, here they are."

"Oh," said Michael, more embarrassed than necessary. "I'm so sorry to have bothered you. I'd forgotten all about that. Please, hold on to them for me until the day of my flight, won't you?"

"Sure, Michael, no problem."

"Again, I apologize for any trouble—"

"Really. It's no trouble. If there's anything else I can do for you—" she began to say, but Michael had already quietly said goodbye and hung up the telephone.

Rebecca grinned like the cat that had swallowed the proverbial canary and replaced the airline tickets where she had found them. She closed the drawer, straightened her desk, removed her white cotton sweater from a hanger on a chrome-plated hook behind the door and turned off the lights before locking up the office.

# 2

Michael spent a quiet evening at home as he most always did. Home was a first-floor apartment in a small condominium near campus. There was only one bedroom. He used the living room as his office and study. The cramped kitchen was located next to the terrace where nothing grew. Nothing had ever grown on that patch of walled-in ground. At least, not during Michael's tenure of ownership.

Dead plants, including philodendrons, ferns and even a lone cactus had turned the patio into a plant cemetery. Michael had left them there, decaying monuments to his failure. He wasn't much good at planting things, let alone nurturing them along to fruition.

Michael stopped working long enough to prepare himself a soft-boiled egg and some toast around seven-thirty that evening. Later, he had some unremarkable red wine while he wrote, in his cramped and scratchy style, on a yellow legal pad.

He neither turned on the television nor touched the radio. In fact, though he possessed one of each, the TV was not plugged into an electrical socket and the radio, though Michael hadn't realized it, was missing.

The television sat huddled in one corner of the living room like a punished schoolboy. It had degenerated, or evolved (depending on how one viewed television) into a scholar's valet. It held a random collection of tomes and papers, most of which, once placed atop the television had never been missed or consulted again.

A lone white sock dangled from the tip of one of the rabbit ear antennae, holding a so far futile and fruitless vigil for its mate.

The radio was in even worse shape having been inadvertently knocked off the kitchen counter one late afternoon by a bag of groceries that Michael had unceremoniously dumped there. Both objects being unable to occupy the same space at the same time, the radio fell off the counter and had become wedged down between the rear of the refrigerator and the kitchen wall.

Michael had not even noticed its absence and probably never would. Oh, sometimes late at night when he came to the kitchen for a snack, he'd hear voices (the on/off switch to the AM/FM radio had been knocked on in its plunge, though the volume was quite low) but he'd always considered that the sounds came from the apartment next door. And the voices were so low that he'd never had need to complain of them to his neighbors.

At the hour of midnight, he turned off all the lights and found his way to the bedroom in the dark. It was no great accomplishment, as it only required, from where he sat, a left turn and a right turn. He'd done it a thousand times. A blind archaeologist could have done it. The worst he could do was run into an errant book or a wall.

He slept without setting an alarm clock. He'd no use for one.

Sometime before three AM, Michael woke and considered the notion of phoning Florida. Not being able to speak with his mother of late had put him off entirely.

It seemed like every time he'd call, she would be out. That wasn't like her. She was active enough for her age, but to be gone all the time? Now, inexplicably, weeks had gone by and he hadn't spoken to her. He dearly missed the talks they always had. Of all the people in the world, Michael was closest to his mother.

Michael debated. It was hours later in Florida, that would make it only about a quarter till six. He knew he shouldn't, but he did. He dialed his parents' house.

"Hello?"

Michael recognized his father's groggy voice. "Hi, Dad, it's me."

"Michael?" said Taft, jerking up in bed. "Are you all right?" he questioned, his voice somewhere between a whisper and a scream.

"Yes, I'm fine. It's nothing like that. I wanted to say hello to Mom."

"Oh. Wow, it's kinda early, early, in the morning isn't it?" said Taft, struggling with his glasses so he could check the clock on the night table.

"I know, Dad. Sorry. I just haven't been able to catch her at home lately. Just a quick hello. Okay?"

"Yeah, sure, sure," agreed his father, though unwillingly. He shook his wife, Marie, who hadn't wakened. "Marie," he whispered, gently tugging her shoulder, "it's Michael. He wants to say hello."

Marie looked at Taft, who only shrugged, as she picked up the receiver. "Hello, Aaron?" she said timidly. Remember, she was the only one who called him Aaron?

Michael's spirits rose the instant he heard his mother's familiar voice. "Hi, Mom," he said. "I wanted to say hello. I've missed you. I know it's early and everything—"

"I miss you too, Aaron."

When Michael moved to California nine years before to take the job with the university it had been hard on everyone, but Michael and his mother found it the hardest. They were the closest mother and son since Mary had Jesus, or so it seemed. Normally, a week didn't go by that they didn't speak on the telephone, until lately that is.

"We're looking forward to your visit. It will be so nice having you home."

"I only wish it could be for longer." Michael was taking five days off counting the weekend. "Well," he said with some hesitation, "I'd better let you get back to sleep. I only wanted to say hello."

"Thank you, Aaron," said his mother, dearly. "I'll sleep better having talked to you."

"Say goodbye to Dad for me."

Marie said she would. She handed the telephone back to her husband who replaced the receiver in its cradle. He hugged his wife and she hugged him right back as best she could.

# 3

At ten o'clock that Florida morning, Taft warmed up the Oldsmobile and helped Marie to the car. Even these few steps were difficult for her.

Taft supposed it was a combination of the malicious cancer spreading through her body and the nearly as malicious drugs that the doctors had been filling her with for the past several months. Soon Taft would have to move the bed into the living room so she could be closer to the kitchen and the bathroom, and the car.

Soon after that, he feared it wouldn't matter.

They arrived at Dr. Richard Cobeur's office at ten-twenty and waited their turn. Taft and Marie hated going to Dr. Cobeur's office for, no matter how cheerfully the doctor and his nurses carried on, and no matter how brightly they decorated the walls with blossoming flowery wallpaper, pastel chairs and sofas, and green plants that hung from baskets whose branches leaped effusively into the air, in spite of all this, Dr. Cobeur's office was a cheerless place.

Because everyone who came into that office knew that this was a place of doom. Of Death. And you had to spell that with a capital D.

Dr. Cobeur was an oncologist and only one of two such specialists in the town of Brooksville, Florida. The other, a Doctor Johnston, was equally competent but Dr. Cobeur's office was closer to their home in the rural reaches just at the eastern edge of Brooksville.

"Kill me."

"What?" asked Taft.

Marie folded her hands across her tiny lap.

Taft squirmed in his chair and looked at the nurse who was safely out of earshot behind the glass partition.

"You might as well kill me."

"What are you talking about?" Taft looked aghast. "You know I'd never do such a thing. You're talking crazy, crazy. I love you. I wouldn't kill you. It's the drugs talking," he said with conviction.

"No," said Marie, "I'm not saying that I think you're trying to kill me. I'm saying that you ought to just do it. You could sneak up behind me and whack me on the back of the head with the shovel out in the tool shed.

"Or," she suggested, "you could wait until I'm sleeping and just put a bag over my head—a plastic one, you know? From the grocery store."

She closed her eyes a moment and trembled. "That wouldn't hurt much, do you think?" she asked, solemnly gazing into her husband's wide eyes. They were eyes of fear and bewilderment.

"Marie..." He put his right arm around his wife's shoulders. He didn't say anything—he didn't want to frighten her— but she felt more bony than ever. Marie's flesh was melting away from her.

Taft remembered the pumpkins he used to carve as a boy with his father, Nathaniel. Taft loved those tiny pumpkin people so much that he could not bear to let them go long after Halloween was over and the last bit of the worst tasting candy in his pillowcase had been eaten, and the last empty wrapper discarded.

His pumpkin would sit on the porch like a brave soldier vowing to fight on through winter, spring, and summer, to fight next year's battle. Though next year's battle never came and a new pumpkin would have to be carved to take the last one's place. Pumpkins don't last long once they've had their insides carved out.

Neither do people, or so it seemed...

"You can go in now," announced the nurse, whose name

was Pamela. Nurse Pamela's crisp blonde hair fell sharply about her neck like a theater curtain. A gold locket gifted to her by her boyfriend hung around her neck. He was a local attorney named Giles Buford.

Taft and Marie had been coming to Dr. Cobeur's office long enough to learn the lineage and social connections of everyone on staff. Marie knew that Buford himself was a transplant from Minneapolis with two sisters and one brother up north. The brother owned a pharmacy and was hoping to retire soon.

Dr. Cobeur had a small staff of only four. Two competent nurses, Pamela and June, and two equally capable girls whose jobs involved shuffling the vast amounts of paper and x-ray film that went in and out of an office even the modest size of Dr. Cobeur's.

The doctor was waiting for them in Examination Room A. It was cold in the room. "Hello, Taft," said Dr. Cobeur.

Taft shook his hand mechanically and said hello.

"How are you, Marie?" the doctor asked with what might have been more than professional interest.

"So-so," answered Marie. She had no misconceptions about her illness. Her stomach cancer had come upon her like a blow to the belly from which she would never recover. It had spread quickly and with murderous intent to her vital organs. She was a walking dead person. It was only a matter of time.

Tick tock, tick tock. Tick Tock of Oz. Today? Tomorrow? Will her life become ever more painful?

Tick tock, tick tock.

Marie tried not to think about it. Didn't even like to be reminded of it, of time, of the future. It was most pleasant when she was all alone in the bedroom, in her bed. How easy it was to close her eyes and think back to better days.

The dreams her memories held.

When her children were young and so then was she. Her husband, a handsome, muscular youth with a world yet to conquer. Now, he seemed so sad and terribly pale. She knew what a toll her illness was taking on him. He wasn't looking so well now himself.

Poor Taft, if only she could make it better for him. Make everything easier for him.

The doctor poked and prodded parts of her body that forty years ago she wouldn't have let her fiancé near. She did a mental shrug. What did it matter anymore?

She had ceased being attractive long ago. What was left of her had been taken by the cancer. It was a stealer not only of flesh but of the sanctity of her dreams...

When she was thirteen, Marie's mother took her ice skating on a frozen lake in St. Clair Shores, Michigan. She and her family lived on a pig farm nearby. An apple orchard sat beside the lake then. Now pricy, custom-built homes occupied only in the summer by the rich filled the space. They had their dreams and she had hers.

Marie fell on the ice and sprained her wrist. She flinched as the pain shot up her elbow. At first, Marie thought she'd only hit her funny bone. That was what she and her friends had called it then. Marie didn't know if funny bones even existed anymore. Her mother, not more than thirty-five then herself (barely Aaron Michael's age now), had scooped her up in her suddenly strong arms and carried her off to the doctor's.

There were no specialists then. Least not so's Marie knew. They only had the one doctor and he took care of everyone. He took care of Marie's wrist and warned her to watch for buried rocks when she skated on the ice. "You're skating on thin ice," he said with mock severity.

Marie and her mother, Betty, both laughed. Marie's mother made her hot Dutch cocoa when they got back home. When her father came back from the factory where he spent the best part of his life, he was all concern and tenderness. He cut Marie's meat for her at dinner, and gave her a big kiss goodnight, and pulled the wool covers up to her throat that night so she wouldn't have to strain herself.

Marie thought that she'd had the finest parents in the world. Though they'd long since moved on, through no fault of their own.

They had been on a different point on the long road to paradise. That was what her father had explained before he died. "There's nothing we can do about it, baby," explained Alan Taggert to his daughter Marie. "I'm on one spot and you're on another, and Mother's on yet another. We're all somewhere along the road.

"We've had this great spot where we got to travel along together for a ways." He paused and closed his eyes. It was getting harder every day to talk. How could talking take so much energy, he wondered? It used to be that he could talk all day and not so much as take an extra breath.

Marie held his hand. That tiny hand in his meant more to him than all the money in the world.

"And who knows," her father said, "maybe we'll all get together someplace else along the way."

Marie cried and put a crooked finger to her eye to catch the tear that had formed.

"Marie," said Taft, "are you all right?"

Marie swallowed, a lump in her throat. Her eyes refused to focus. She knew the doctor was looking at her. She shook her head. "Yes, I'm fine."

# 4

Michael struggled with consciousness. He hated these department meetings and, try as he would, staying awake was a battle.

"—and I've requested state funding which would allow us to conduct a joint physical lab with the California Highway Patrol on recent innovations in forensics," announced Dr. Amil Canar.

Canar was the resident physical anthropologist though lately he seemed to be more interested in crime and crime solving, and seemed to spend half of his time and resources playing anthro-detective. He had a skin condition that reminded Michael for all the world of an ectoplasmic pseudopodium.

And how could anyone have dirty protoplasm? Didn't the man ever use a washcloth? Or swipe his teeth with a toothbrush for that matter?

Michael was fairly certain that it was Dr. Canar who had also attempted to blackball him when his tenure came up for university review. At least that had been intimated to him by his colleagues. And he'd be the first to admit that this might be coloring his opinion of the man.

"Wonderful," said Dr. Randall Cane, clapping his dry white hands together, clearly satisfied with the outcome of the meeting. Cane's hands looked to Michael like two dry chalkboard erasers. He wouldn't have been surprised if chalk dust had come spouting out in cloudy white puffs while the man clapped.

Cane continued, "I suggest we adjourn unless someone has something further to add?" He scanned the room with the rise of a set of eyebrows which clung to his forehead like a pair of shiny black leeches of the bloodsucking Australasian variety.

A consensus of noes echoed around the glossy dark oblong table absolutely filling the tiny faculty conference room. It was Wednesday afternoon, after all, and most of the faculty wanted to get home.

Michael, too, was anxious to be gone. He had yet to pack and his flight was for tomorrow afternoon. He had a class to teach in the morning, and would be cutting it close at that.

"So," said Bob Bandry, catching up to Michael in the narrow hallway outside his office, "what did you think?"

"What do you mean, Bob?" asked Michael. Robert Bandry was a social anthropologist and the closest thing Michael had to a friend on or off campus.

Bob's most significant feature was his nose. A noble proboscis with a noticeable leftward tilt. Michael knew this was the result of a misunderstanding between Bob and a Maori tribesman concerning one of the tribesman's overly flirtatious daughters.

Before the misunderstanding could be resolved, Bob had ended up with a busted nose. But all's well that ends well, as the saying goes. Bob and his tribesman assailant, Tirakahurangi, were now on the best of terms, penpals even. In his last letter to Bob, Tirak wrote that his flirtatious, and very single, daughter was planning a trip to the States. Michael warned Bob to be careful, but the advice bounced off. Bob was not the cautious type and said the girl would be no problem.

Michael had no way of judging the veracity of Bob's claim. The problem Michael so keenly foresaw was that Bob's wife, Gwen, was very much the jealous type.

"I mean about the old man's speech about our not requesting enough state and federal funding—" The *old man* was Randall Cane whom some say had been on earth long enough to qualify for apostlehood.

"Oh." Michael hadn't really been paying attention. He had grown disheartened as he came to be a faculty member to discover that there was an extraordinary amount of politicking taking place at a so-called place of higher education. Nearly the whole lot of them were petty as middle schoolers. As a holder of a tenured position, one would have to pretty well run amuck decapitating fellow faculty members or defrocking coeds to lose one's job, and yet still there were those who vied for position and prestige.

"What can we do?" Michael shrugged. "I can't request money I don't need."

"But that's just Randall's point. If you don't keep requesting more and more, someone else is going to get your share and then you'll end up getting less and less."

"Maybe," replied Michael, "but if we keep requesting more money, we'll have to find something to spend it on and that would just create more work and more headaches. How do we separate the real work from the make-work?"

It was Professor Bandry's turn to shrug. "Who's to say? When I started out," Bob was sixteen years Michael's senior, "it was publish or perish but there wasn't anyone telling us that we had to go out and panhandle as much money as we could from the government. Now, it's expected of us." He patted Michael's shoulder paternally. "All part of the job, Michael."

Michael had no reply to this.

"Let's forget it," said Bob. "Come on, I'll buy you lunch and you can make me green with envy telling me about this vacation to Florida you're planning."

# 5

Rebecca looked at her watch, looked at the door, then looked at her watch again. It was nearly six o'clock and Michael had still not left his office. She knew he was in there because several times she'd sneaked down the hall and checked. He was buried in his work and hadn't moved in hours. Yet Rebecca had resolved to wait for him.

She knew that he would almost certainly come down the hall past her office, when he did go, and she was waiting, however impatiently, to speak with him. She could easily have gone to his office to talk, but she didn't want to look eager or pushy. Michael was the type of man who was going to have to be handled delicately, gently. Oscar Wilde and fine china.

At half past the hour, finally, she heard him securing his door. She grabbed a pen and acted officious. Her heart raced. She sensed his footsteps coming up the tiled corridor. She recognized his distinctive shuffling gait.

Michael froze in the frame of her door when she called out. "Hi!" Her voice rang out like a sniper's shot. Had she sounded too loud? Too anxious? Too late to worry about that now.

Michael turned. "Hello. Working late?"

"Just finishing up," Rebecca said with well-rehearsed nonchalance. She dropped her pen in a University of California ceramic mug and rose from her chair. "I'll walk out with you," she added boldly. "Hold on. Let me lock up."

Michael stood by uncomfortably, shifting his weight from foot to foot, his briefcase dangling awkwardly at his side. Already he fretted over having to make small talk with this woman whom he barely knew.

Rebecca turned out the lights and twisted the key in the

lock. She dropped the weighty set of keys into her purse and draped the purse strap over her right shoulder. "You're working pretty late yourself," she said, walking slowly beside him.

"Yes. I'm afraid I won't get much work done while I'm away."

Rebecca nodded. "Don't forget, I've still got your airline tickets."

"Yes, I hope I don't forget."

"Maybe I should pin them to your jacket."

Michael blushed and Rebecca regretted her little joke. "I'm only teasing," she said. She lightly touched his arm and then drew back. She didn't want to scare him off.

"I know," he lied.

"Listen," said Rebecca as they stood, awkward as two strangers, together on the grey steps outside the anthropology building, "you'll need a ride to the airport tomorrow. I could take you. If you like," she added hastily.

"Doctor Cane said it would be okay. In fact, he thought it was a good idea." He had said Michael might very well get lost trying to reach LAX on his own.

Last year, Michael and Dr. Cane had gone to a symposium together in Denver. Michael had driven them to the Los Angeles International Airport and gone the wrong way down a one-way street. While there had been no wrecks, only a couple very near misses, they'd missed their flight and Dr. Cane had missed his panel.

This was a tale that came up typically at university parties and holiday affairs. Michael had long ago grown weary of hearing about it.

"No, thank you," said Michael. "It's a long drive for you to have to make. I thought I would drive my car and leave it at the airport. It's only for a few days."

"It's not too far at all," answered Rebecca. "I have a sister who lives down in Santa Monica. I go out there almost every weekend. It wouldn't be any trouble at all. Besides," she admitted, "I more or less promised Doctor Cane that I'd take care of you."

Michael didn't know what to say. "How would I get home again?" he asked, trying to discourage the young secretary from an uncomfortable predicament for them both.

"No problem. I'll pick you up when you get back. Like I said, it's all arranged."

Michael shook his head. "Well. . ."

"Great," said Rebecca. She tugged his sleeve. "I know you have class until eleven-thirty and your flight leaves at three-fifteen, so if you want, we can stop for lunch on the way to the airport. My treat."

And with that she turned with a grin and a wave and headed to her car.

Michael stared at her for a moment afterward and then headed in the opposite direction to his own vehicle. This was a red ten-speed bicycle that he rode to the university as often as he could. He unlocked the front tire from the bike rack and strapped his briefcase to the handle bars with a bungee cord. Rebecca's little Toyota was already far ahead and shrinking fast.

Michael pedaled steadily.

# 6

Detroit was bustling now. And though Taft and Aaron Michael Hart did not yet exist, Nathaniel could feel their presence in the air. It hung there like dusty molecules carrying a scent of hope. His shoes were dirty and could have used resoling. He didn't have the money for this and had to make due with stiff paper tucked between his socks and the street. He'd discovered that it worked best with a bit of wax paper in between layers as well. This helped to keep the moisture out.

Nathaniel Hart walked the streets of his lower Detroit neighborhood with possessive authority. These streets were his home just as much as the tiny brownstone where he dwelled when he wasn't busy trying to keep bread on the table.

At the turn of the century, Detroit was going places. It was Saturday and the streets were full. Home to over a quarter of a million souls (well mostly souled— there were always a few empties lying around) and in a hundred years there would be millions more.

Who knew what the percentage of empties would be then?

Nathaniel Hart worked in the Olds Motor Works. He worked the assembly line. Ransom Olds, the company founder, had given him the job personally. The two young men had known each other from the days before Ransom Eli Olds became a millionaire industrialist and was strictly an equally hard-working automobile mechanic.

Often, Ransom would frequent the beer gardens where Nathaniel played the accordion (with great dexterity for little pay). Eventually, Ransom went on to establish the first automobile factory and the first such factory to use an assembly line.

Nathaniel, though skilled at both the chromatic and piano accordion, was quickly convinced that he could earn better and steadier pay working in the factory.

His family's welfare improved, though Nathaniel was unable to give up his muse. He worked sixteen hours a day in the factory and closed the beer gardens at night with the melodies he manufactured there.

He sang songs about everything, people, places, his mood of the day, a dog whose path he might have crossed. Once he even wrote three verses about a favorite urinal. He wrote about Harriet Elizabeth Beecher Stowe, who wrote Oldtown Folks, a book which Nathaniel's mother, Sarah, had read when it rolled off the presses in 1869. The year that he, Nathaniel was composed himself.

He was born to the world in 1870 and he used to tell people (so's they'd know) that 1870 was the very same year that Sumba Island, a not inconsequential island in the Malay Archipelago was celebrating the four-year anniversary of its coming under direct Dutch control (well, it was an anniversary for some).

If you'd ever seen a piece of sandalwood or sniffed on a burning lump of sandalwood incense, there was a good chance that it had come from the forests of Sumba. It was no wonder that some people shook their heads when they saw Nathaniel coming.

Nate stopped at the grocer's and bought a bag of peaches. They were fresh and came from New Brooklyn, New Jersey. Nate said that if you ate enough Jersey peaches, you'd end up speaking New Brooklynese.

Nate was not playing checkers today. He held his cribbage board under his arm. He'd fashioned it himself from an old pine two-by-four and a nail that he'd used to gouge out the holes (two rows of thirty holes for each player and one at the end) and a couple of pegs (guitar) to keep score.

Sir John Suckling swallowed some horrible poison in the summer of 1642 and Paris buried him. Perhaps if Sir John had let his friend, Sir Tom Wentworth, rot a little longer in the Tower of London instead of attempting an ill-fated rescue, he'd have lived to play cribbage a little longer. He could have retired to the sunny, dry coast of Spain collecting the revenues from his vast English estates and enjoyed the notoriety that came with having invented such a charming diversion.

Cribbage was Sir John Suckling's game. Politics was another, though he played it with far less skill. And Sir Thomas Wentworth, First Earl of Strafford, who'd done so much for his England, was accused, by jealous detractors, of treason and, though it was never proved, the Long Parliament saw no reason that this should deter them from sentencing him to death and beheading him.

This they did.

Nate kicked the toe of his left shoe against the dry pavement. The cardboard was slipping and a good kick realigned it without his having to stop and pull off his shoe. He turned and crossed Lafayette Street.

Of course, Lafayette had never known Sieur Antoine de la Mothe Cadillac, who had given Detroit its original appellation of Pontchartrain d'Etroit—as French military commander, Cadillac was prone to naming settlements and anything else that he saw fit. With the written permission of the King of France, Louis the XIV, Sir Cadillac officially founded Pontchartrain d'etroit in 1701 —exactly two hundred years (as near as can tell) to the time that Nate was crossing Lafayette Street (Lafayette, of course, had come by much later in our story and so had to settle for having a street named for himself).

Nathaniel, of course, to be fair, had a child named for himself (a last name anyway) though he would not be born for nearly twenty years more and he in turn would have another son, and his name would be Aaron Michael.

The good Sieur Antoine de la Mothe Cadillac, later governor of Louisiana territory, returned to France in 1717 and didn't have to live with the name he'd given to this Michigan city. In fact, someone went so far as to name an automobile in his honor, the Mothe (Well, something like that).

# 7

Rebecca drove a Toyota that was built in several places excluding Detroit and Michael found it to be only slightly cramped for leg room. Nate's cribbage board, somewhat worn, was tucked away somewhere in a box somewhere in a corner (also somewhere) of the attic in Taft Hart's house. If there were any such thing as time travel that cribbage board knew the principles involved.

"You really didn't have to go to all this trouble," said Michael, balancing his briefcase on his lap. The car hung to the road with the exception of the wobble caused by passing semis with loaded down trailers (probably not filled with cribbage boards).

"No trouble at all." Rebecca turned and gave him a reassuring smile.

Shouldn't she be watching the road? he thought. Rebecca's skin was lightly bronzed and her brown hair seemed to shine. She was dressed in a summer frock decorated with a dazzling pattern of yellow woodsorrels; though autumn had settled in and even California noticed the change.

Rebecca glanced in the rearview mirror and apprised her chances before swinging into the far right lane with only a hint of rebound. "I know a great place in Oxnard," she said. "You'll love the food."

Michael started to tell her that it wasn't necessary to stop for lunch but found himself unable to tell her so and doubted if it would affect her actions much if he did.

Oxnard was a verdant arena of farmland being squeezed slowly to death by creeping civilization. Once known for its sugar beets and being the home of the world's second largest sugar processing plant, beets had come to be replaced by a variety of vegetables and fruits, such as the fields of strawberry that lined the Ventura Freeway.

Rebecca dove off the freeway, passed rows of strawberry plants and soon was coursing down Oxnard Boulevard. Traffic was heavy. Must have weighed a ton.

"Watch for it," said Rebecca. "I think it's on your side of the street," She drove with one hand and pointed across his face with the other. "It's called the Golden Apple."

Michael did as he was directed. Hardware stores, grocery stores, shoe stores, one shoe repair store, two baseball card stores. "There it is." He stuck out his hand. "That's it."

The sign hung above the lintel appeared to have been painstakingly hand-painted. One large plate glass window, with a round stained-glass design of reds and blues and evergreens in a lead frame suspended in the middle of that window, let the sun peek inside. And though the sun was currently arcing in like a torch, the curtains remained defiantly open.

With all the street parking occupied, Rebecca leapt up the nearest alley and slid the car along a wall that looked so ancient that the Romans might have left it there.

"Sorry. You'll have to climb out my side, I'm afraid," apologized Rebecca, after assessing the situation.

"Right." The Toyota rested so close to the wall that Michael wasn't able to get so much as a foot out the passenger side door. He tucked his briefcase under the front seat (so it went only part way) and climbed over the four-speed gear knob between the two seats with great care. Michael was glad that he'd decided against wearing a suit and tie to the airport.

Rebecca held the door open for him as he clambered out.

A pungent amalgamation of odors struck his nostrils as they entered and seated themselves at a table near the window. Michael quickly felt like he was being slow-fried under a magnifying glass. A bead of ticklish perspiration sprouted under his lip.

The faded, red-speckled Formica-and-steel table and the

pink plastic-covered chairs all appeared to have been purchased third-hand at a second-hand store.

After a skeptical look at the dubious menu, Michael ordered a barbecued tofu burger and a tofu shake. Carob flavored. The woman behind the counter claimed they didn't have chocolate. In fact, when Michael requested a chocolate malt, the young woman gaped at him as if he'd just committed sacrilege in St. Paul's Cathedral by pissing in the baptismal font or lighting up a cigarette with a votive candle or something equally as blasphemous. Michael quickly apologized and ordered the carob tofu shake in its stead. A drink which the young woman assured him was far healthier for him than the chocolate.

Albert Einstein (in portrait form) hung on the wall behind the counter, protected from smoke and grease in a black-edged glass picture frame. Beneath the great man, in gold lettering, was a quote from the mathematician espousing vegetarianism.

"Nice," declared Michael as he ate his sandwich off the recycled plastic tray provided with lunch. He bit into his sandwich and took a long slow pull on his tofu shake. To his surprise, it was palatable.

"I'm glad you like it, Michael." Rebecca ordered some sort of lunch salad full of exotic vegetables (it looked to Michael like someone had diced up a box of 64-color Crayola crayons and set the result on a bed of romaine lettuce) and red zinger tea. "I know it's not fancy or anything, but it's delicious and healthy."

"Yes, it is that," agreed Michael, contemplating the tofu curds floating in his drink.

Albert Einstein gazed out from behind the glass partition separating him from the world below. If only one of those lackadaisical waitresses would clean the frame once in a while, he was sure his eyesight wouldn't be bothering him so much.

In between his work on relativity and his writings on unified fields and brownian movement was one tiny theory that Einstein had kept all to himself. That theory allowed him to exist inside any picture that existed of himself, including the one now hanging on a four-penny nail over the crusted and fingermarked polemoniums embellished wallpaper that in turn adorned (some waitresses said 'held together') the Golden Apple restaurant.

Albert called it the photodimension. Though sometimes he got tired of it and called it garbage.

Worst of all were those pictures of him tucked inside thousands and millions of encyclopedias. Most of the time, he couldn't see anything out of them at all. It was either too dark or he was staring at some dry facts like the fact that Einbeck (famous for its beer) had once been the home of a cathedral whose chapel purportedly contained the blood of the Saviour.

What rubbish. These days he knew there were many kids running around in T-shirts and sweatshirts with pen and ink drawings of himself on the frontside. Albert wished he could live through them but, as yet, this had proved impossible. Only photographs would do.

Einstein thought fondly of Munich, once his home. For a time, after a popular biography on him had been published, he had been able to stare at the lofty and provoking Liebfrauenkirche, (a book vendor maintained a stall under a tall oak near the church and kept Einstein's book in a spot of prominence there). He gazed often upon that church and frequently mused what might have stood on that earth hundreds of years before. Hardworking laborers built the church built in the fifteenth century and no photographs of Einstein had existed then. Else he would return to that time and stand on that (perhaps) barren soil (farmland maybe) and imagine that cathedral one day popping into existence. And, in imagining it, perhaps it could be he who made it exist.

Rise, Liebfrauenkirche, he might say with a commanding gesture of his arms. Einstein feared he was becoming a soddy sentimentalist. Perhaps he should take up the accordion? After all, it was a good German instrument. The chromatic accordion had been birthed in Berlin in 1822. A mere babe-in-the-woods in the world of musical instruments. He would have to give the notion further thought.

Jacob's Ladder climbed the walls.

At the airport, Michael handed his plane ticket to the person in charge of such affairs. She took receipt of it as if it were the key to millions of Swiss francs locked away in an unnumbered bank account.

"Well," began Michael, with a palpable awkwardness, "thank you for the ride, Rebecca."

"You're welcome." She struggled to stay close as boarding passengers wormed their way between them, heading through security.

"Well," muttered Michael once again. It seemed to be the pinnacle of his eloquency.

Rebecca leaned forward slowly, as if she were leaning into a bubble that might burst at any moment at any pressure, and kissed Michael delicately on his smooth cheek. She drew back and smiled. "Better hurry," she said, wiping a thread from his lapel "or you'll miss your plane."

With that, she gave Michael (who seemed to be suffering from the Medusa Effect or some strange onset of a nervous disorder) a light push that headed him down the passengers-only ramp and onto the airplane.

From there, a handy stewardess led him to his seat in business class. Another sheep sent safely along his way.

# 8

"So," said Taft, "how was your flight. Your mother is dying."

Was that how he was supposed to say it?

Shit, shit. Things had never been good between he and Michael and now he had to be the one to tell his son that his mother, whom he loved dearly, was dying. Sonofabitch. How was he supposed to tell the kid that? Let alone tell Michael that everybody else in the family knew about it and had been keeping it a secret from him for nearly four months.

Michael had never been a strong boy emotionally. That had been the excuse for not mentioning the news to him initially.

"Don't tell Aaron. Promise me," pleaded Marie. "It will kill him."

Taft ceded.

"I'm sure I'll get better," said Marie. Better never came. Oh, there had been bright optimistic moments where the cancer had seemed to go into remission. But each time had been a cruel hoax and the cancer had come back strong. Now, with Michael's unexpected visit, the news wouldn't wait. Marie was too far along in her illness for it to be otherwise.

Taft paced outside his car, the Saint Petersburg-Clearwater International Airport hanging like a menace above him. If only one of the girls had flown down from Detroit it would have been so much easier. He steeled himself with a deep breath and went in to find his son.

# 9

Michael plucked his single black suitcase from the luggage carousel and fought his way through the pressing herd of fellow passengers. He spotted his father before his father spotted him. Michael set his briefcase down next to his suitcase, leaving both carelessly unattended, and walked briskly toward Taft. "Dad," he said, his voice barely carrying through the few feet of air between them.

Taft heard the call of "Dad" and recognized his son's voice. "Michael!" he greeted in a voice trebly amplified in comparison to his offspring's. He changed directions and loped ahead to his son. Though Michael had long ago exceeded him in height, Taft managed to bear hug his son and lift him off the ground. "It's good to see you, Michael."

"You too, Dad." Michael looked around expectantly. "Where's Mother?"

"Oh, ah," Taft sputtered. He hadn't been expecting to get right to the bone this quickly. "She's waiting at home."

It was true, after all. "You know how women are—always fussing over every little thing. I expect she wants the house to look great great."

Michael smiled, though his disappointment was clear. "That's okay, we'll be there soon." Something nagged at the corner of his mind but it was too small for his notice.

"Sure sure," said Taft. "Those your bags?" He pointed to Michael's two pieces.

"Yes, sir."

Taft picked them up, one in each hand. "I got 'em," he said. Michael would always be his little boy needing a helping hand.

"Come on, Dad, I can take them."

"Nope, I got 'em."

"At least give me one of them—"

"Relax relax," said Taft. "You've had a long flight. You must be tired. And as soon as we step out those doors, you're about to be blasted with good old Florida humidity. Ninety proof. You've been in California so long, you've probably forgotten what that's like."

Michael grinned tolerantly, if unbelievingly. The two men stepped out the automatic doors and into the sunlight and, for just an instant, Michael had to fight the instinct to start paddling to stay afloat. The air was so wet he was nearly forced to swim.

Taft Hart popped open the trunk of his white Oldsmobile and deposited his son's bags therein. "How's everything going at the university?" Taft asked as he headed down through St. Petersburg, a town which had (by coincidence mind you) been incorporated in 1903, the same year as Oxnard, California. Perhaps the legal profession was running a special on town incorporation papers that year.

"Nothing much. It becomes pretty much a routine what with classes and all." Michael gazed lazily out the side window as they glided over Old Tampa Bay on the Howard Frankland Bridge. He didn't know who Howard Frankland was or why he'd come to have a bridge with his name on it.

Soon they were in and out of Tampa and heading north up lonely State Road 41 to Brooksville.

The sky was feeling blue, the grass was looking green. Verdant fields and moon-eyed cows dotted the vista. The air smelled redolent with the scent of autumn.

Yes, it was a great day for war.

And, of course, Taft Hart waited until the last possible moment to let blow the first salvo. No preliminary skirmishes, no harsh words exchanged at a distance, no battle cry of mournful and delirious trumpets. Just a quick deep slice to the heart, meant to be painless and failing sadly and extremely.

Taft brought the Oldsmobile to a halt in the front drive and turned off the engine. The car shivered to a halt. "Son," said Taft, gripping his knees, "there's something I've got to tell you—"

"Yes?" Michael looked at his father.

The Franks didn't mean to stir up trouble. Some say it was their nature. Some say it was all Clovis' fault. Instead of divvying up his kingdom amongst his four squabbling, ingrate sons he should have set up a republic. Or perhaps some form of agrarian Communism. Of course, this would have hurt Karl Marx's chance at the history books considerably.

One cannot fault Clovis entirely. By Frank standards he was a good king even if he did convert to Christianity causing all his Frankish followers to have to change their religious icons at frightfully low exchange rates. He overthrew Syagrius, the last of the Roman governors of Gaul, smote hordes of Burgundians, Visigoths, and Allamani. And he reportedly slew the great Visigothic king, Alaric II, with his own capable hands on the fields of Vouille near Poitiers in France (which is a great place to go if you need pantyhose).

The cathedral at Poitiers is also interesting and, though it was built in 1162, it is no match for the Liebfrauenkirche, or such was Einstein's opinion. The cathedral, located smack in the frenchiest of French parts, was built curiously enough by the English and a certain Henry II (a querulous rascal best known for defeating Eleanor of Aquitaine [in bed] and begetting Richard the Lion-Hearted) takes credit for that.

The Franks had the last laugh and named a whole country for themselves. Some say the name should have been the discretion of the Romans who had laid first claim to the fine, fertile lands. But the Franks apparently had a better marketing group and their lobby was certainly better greased. Like bovines, they ran about the land in tribal herds, sequestering and bootying to their hearts delight.

The cows on the farms surrounding Brooksville only chewed the spongy sod and shat aimlessly. They rarely even spoke to one another—without reading material or even television, they had soon run out of fresh topics for conversation and their oral traditions were simply horrendous. I mean, how much information can you hand down cow generation after cow generation using just the one word, moo?

Moo.

"Mom's sick."

"What do you mean?" asked Michael. Sternocleidomastoid muscles flexed and unflexed.

Taft stared out the front window towards the house. Marie must've drawn the curtains again. The trim could use painting. "She's sick," he repeated. "I just wanted to let you know so's you won't be," he paused, "shocked, when you see her."

Michael stiffened and stared with growing incomprehension at his father. "What do you mean sick?" His eyes were dark as storm clouds.

"Son," said Taft, "don't go getting all upset now. We're doing everything we can for your mother. She's got the best doctors—"

"What's wrong with her?" Michael said loudly. He was already half out the car door, his body a contradiction of tense actions.

"Marie has cancer," explained Taft, his voice chasing his son like a tailwind.

Michael ran to the house.

"Stomach cancer," whispered Taft. He gripped the rubbery steering wheel for support and for a moment the world seemed to sway under his feet.

Perspiration drained from Taft like water from a cartoon character shot full of holes. By the time Taft found the strength to remove himself from the car, he must have contributed about five pounds of water to the already heavy air.

Taft went with great foreboding into his house. It was quiet. He didn't have to look. He knew where his son would be. He would be in the bedroom with his mother. Taft went to the kitchen and made himself a ham sandwich. The ham was fresh from the grocery. It looked good. He inhaled. It smelled so so good. He laid the mustard on thick and bit off big chunks of bread and meat and chewed slowly. He stood over the kitchen counter as he ate. He washed it all down with an ice-cold glass of whole milk. He would pay for it later. Life was like that.

Michael joined him.

"Like a sandwich?"

"No, thanks," answered Michael somewhat guardedly. He looked out the kitchen window and studied the flowers blossoming in the yard. The homes here sat on quarter-acre lots and his mother had always been proud of her flower gardens. Even when they lived up in Michigan, her flowers were the best and lasted the latest into the season before winter came and covered them with cold, gentle snowflakes.

"Can I get you anything?" asked Taft.

"No, thanks."

"Okay. If you get hungry, help yourself."

"You should have told me."

Taft sighed like a dying dog. "She made me promise." Taft recognized that this was pretty much his time of reckoning with his son. "It wasn't easy for us to keep it from you. Your mother didn't want you to worry. She thinks you're too sensitive, too delicate. Your sisters love your mom, too, but this sort of thing doesn't affect them like it does you—"

"They knew?" said Michael, turning on his father with renewed anger, a dying fire finding a new fuel source.

Taft nodded somberly. "Yeah." Pause. "Yeah."

"So everybody in the fucking world knew that Mom was dying except me?" He swore in anger, his voice rising like a squall. He spat out another line of invective, though he was not a person to swear. "Is that it? Is that what you're telling me?"

"Michael," implored Taft, "calm down. I'm, I'm sorry it had to be this way."

"It didn't have to be this way," retorted Michael. "Somebody could have told me!"

Taft took the blows as they came. But he didn't hang his head. He took every blow to his heart, one by one; blows from the hammer, as they came. He was a father. It was his duty.

"Aaron!" cried Marie. "What are you doing?"

Marie had pulled herself up out of bed and managed to put on her good robe, the flannel one which Taft had bought her in Kentucky on a trip five years previously. Handmade by a woman local to the region. He had purchased it for her at a consignment craft shop near Prestonsburg.

Michael, hurt and confounded, stopped mid-sentence.

"How dare you speak to your father that way."

"Marie," said Taft. He'd run over to his ailing wife and was holding her steady, one hand around her waist, the other supporting her elbow. "It's all right. You shouldn't have got out of bed."

"Hush now, both of you," said Marie, her voice as stern as a hurricane buffeting the gulf coast shore.

"I'm sorry," said Michael. He could have been a plastic balloon pricked and deflated.

"You should be," berated Marie. "I told your father not to tell you. I didn't want you to worry. And look how you're carrying on already. You act as if I'm already dead or something. Well, I'm not Aaron Michael Hart. I am not dead. So, how about being civil and spending some time with me? And your father. And we'll have no more of these criminations."

Michael bit down on the inside of his cheek.

She took her son's hand in her right and held her husband's right arm locked in her left. "I want to walk in my garden."

The two men led her tenderly down the back steps.

Morning-glories in pinks, whites and blues dotted the path. "The horsemint is holding up well," remarked Marie, stooping as best she could and running two tactile fingers over a healthy leaf.

There was a time when she would carefully pick and dry the leaves for tea. The tea was supposed to have a medicinal effect. Perhaps she should try some now. No, it was probably too late for that.

She gazed out over her tiny plot of land. In the summer, there would be Black-eyed Susans (named for Olof Rudbeck a Swedish botanist at the University of Upsala who died in

1702, one year after the founding of Pontchartrain d'etroit) and geraniums.

"I think I should sit down," said Marie, fighting back a wave of nausea and dizziness.

"Let's go back to the house," Taft suggested.

"No, I want to stay outside for a time."

"I'll get you a chair," Michael offered.

"Stay," said Marie, a weak yet commanding grip on his arm. "I want to sit on the grass. I want to feel the earth."

Neither man said a word. They helped Marie. She sat down slowly and sighed when she touched the ground. "The shade here," she said, "between the sweet gum and the live oak is the best. Certain trees, you know," she explained, "combine to create the best shade, the best coverage, the best color and somehow each combination creates its own kind of shade. Live oak and sweet gum, that's the best for me."

"Back home," she went on, "when I was a girl, we had a stand of boxelder and gray birch out in front of the house. They produced great shade. I used to play between those trees for hours unending during the summertime. Mother would bring me fresh lemonade that she made herself, not like that powdery stuff so many folks make today. She said if I didn't drink, I'd dry up like an old leaf."

Marie pattered her son's hand. "You should have seen it, Aaron," she said fondly. "You would have enjoyed it there."

"Yes, Mother." Michael envisioned his mother as a child, healthy, bright and happy.

# 10

Marie went to bed early that night. Taft slept fitfully beside her. Michael stared at the ceiling in the spare room. He felt disoriented and confused. And a little betrayed. He was angry with his father most of all. When he slept at all, it was deep and dreamless.

Marie slept peacefully, for peace had come to her. The engine of her dreams drove her, majestically, on her way to paradise. The road was long. She passed her mother and father and sisters and nearly all her friends from as long ago as early childhood. She saw her old best friend Kathy, whose family had the place next to her own when they were children exploring the universe together from their mutual backyards in rural Michigan, the lumbering family dog of uncertain breed and strong heart whom she'd named Tiggy, and the great-aunt, long since dead with a face like a Bedlington terrier who used to sit with her and taught her to play the piano.

There were great looming forests of trees, a stand of three-hundred-foot-tall sweetgums (the General Shermans of sweetgums) covered a hillside and their scent filled the air. Every house she'd ever lived in lined a street shaded with boxelder, and a sunflower was painted on every mailbox. She grinned like a child (the child she'd always been though her body had aged) and clasped her hands gleefully.

Marie didn't feel the pain in her belly that fought at her tooth and nail. It couldn't reach her here. She was home now. Pain and death were not allowed to enter this world. Inside, nailed to a wall of each house, in gold-painted oak frames beneath the stairways, stood photographs of the great man himself, Albert Einstein.

Marie died in the night.

She never knew it. In fact, if you could have put through a phone call to her or forwarded a missive via Western Union, she would have said, with surprise, that you were certainly mistaken and that she was most definitely not dead!

Marie did not know death. She pulled a fresh carrot from the damp earth beside her house and rinsed it under the spigot. The water ran down her forearms and her legs. The water was cool. The carrot was sweet.

# 11

Taft opened his eyes with a start. It was hard to sleep anymore. He fought down the urge to vomit. He sat up and angled his pillow beneath his back. Sweat limned his face. Each day was getting harder. He'd have to call his friend, Benji, in the morning. He looked through the dim light of night at Marie lying beside him, sleeping; her nostrils flaring slightly with each gentle breath, serenely. Sleep had become her refuge and he did not begrudge her that. It allowed her to escape the pain that he knew she was feeling.

Taft turned back the covers and twisted his legs off the bed, feeling for his slippers with his cold, bare feet; all with one smooth motion. His damp cotton pajamas clung to his old skin like wet tissue paper. He quietly slipped from the room, unable to sleep any longer. Taft was lucky to get four hours of sleep a night. The days just kept getting longer.

He crept down the hallway through the dark passage that he knew so well and stopped at the door to Michael's room. He put an ear to the hollow-core door and listened to his son's breathing as it came steadily, like waves pounding the shore. It had been ages since he had listened to his son's breathing. When Michael was an infant Taft would hold the boy in his arms for hours on end while he slept. And Taft had been as comforted by those moments as the child had been.

He went to the kitchen, took a glass from the draining rack in the sink and poured himself a quarter of a cup of tap water. It was barely cool. He carried the glass to the Florida room and sat bolt upright in his recliner. Usually he read or watched television during these lost hours of the night. Tonight he sat in the unlit house and waited. For what he did not know.

# 12

Marie rose from her matrimonial bed, in a swirl of pearl white dressing gown and well-worn slippers. She stole soundlessly down the hallway and ran through the house, past Taft who sat in his favorite chair and disappeared out the back door heading toward the garden.

"Marie!" yelled Taft with such a start that he dropped his water glass. The glass hit the carpet and rolled to a halt beside the magazine rack, its harmless contents seeping into the nether side of the floor.

"Marie!" he called again, more urgently, panic in his voice. "What are you doing? Come back!"

Taft jumped from the chair and ran toward the kitchen. "Marie?" He fumbled in the darkness for the light switch and, when his fingers found it, the room was bathed in fluorescence. "Marie?"

She wasn't there and the kitchen door was locked and the chain in place. He looked out the window and thought that he saw something white flash like a sheet dancing in the wind between the trees. "Marie!"

He twisted the lock on the doorknob and jerked the back door open, ripping the flimsy chain from the doorframe. Taft stumbled down the steps and hurried out to the dark garden. Barefoot. Somehow he'd lost his slippers. The ground was cool and damp between his toes. The moon had disappeared. Where the fuck did the moon go? "Marie!"

Michael woke without knowing why. He opened his eyes. It was still dark. He cocked his head and listened. Had he heard someone shouting? He held his breath and strained to hear. A crash broke the silence. A burglar? Had someone broken into the house?

Michael leapt from his bed and clumsily pulled on his trousers. He opened the bedroom door cautiously and tiptoed down the hallway. He heard shouting and saw a light coming from the kitchen. Michael peeked around the kitchen entryway and nearly jumped out of his skin when he saw the kitchen door hanging ajar and the door chain dangling and broken.

"Marie!"

Michael heard his father's voice calling plaintively in the distance.

Rushing out, Michael found his father, knee-deep in morning-glories. The old man looked frightened and dazed. "Dad?"

Taft turned and stared at his son almost as if he did not see him. Almost as if he did not want to.

"Dad?" repeated Michael. "Are you all right?"

"Michael?" said Taft, a dazed countenance pressed upon his face. "Michael."

"Yes, Dad, it's me. I'm here, right here. Are you all right?" Michael reached an arm out to his father and gripped him by the shoulder, as if snatching him back from the dark and invisible evil that threatened them both.

"Marie—" Taft, a puzzled expression passing over his face, surveyed the night.

"Come on, Dad," said Michael. He looked at his father's wet, bare feet. "Let's get you inside."

Taft allowed himself to be pulled along, though he twisted his head backward with every step, in a vain effort to discover his missing wife.

Michael closed the kitchen door and sat his father down at the kitchen table. He fished out the kettle and filled it from the faucet with water enough for two. He set the kettle on the front burner of the electric stove and switched it on high. The coils glowed orange.

Outside, a Chuck-will's widow (Caprimulgus vociferus) jarred the night with its lament. And though Aristotle would have cautioned all the goats to run inside their barns to save their teats from this goatsucker, the Chuck-will gave goats nary a thought. In fact, he thoroughly preferred insects, and the codling moth, though rare, was a personal favorite.

Michael tossed a tea bag apiece into two pale blue china cups and set them on the table. He brought the sugar jar and placed it before his father. "Come on, Dad," he said, "drink. It'll warm you up." Michael dropped a teaspoonful of sugar into the bottom of his own cup and stirred.

Michael added sugar to his father's cup and removed the tea bags from both. He wrapped the tea bags meticulously around the spoon and drained them by tugging on the strings. He pushed his father's cup closer to the edge of the table. Mist rose toward Taft's chin. "Drink," he said once more.

Taft stared at his cup. Steam whirled into the air like dragon's breath. "I saw Marie," he whispered. "She went outside but I couldn't catch her."

Michael stared at his father. "What are you talking about?"

Taft held the beechwood table in his weakening grip. "She ran past me—in the living room. I was sitting there. Couldn't sleep."

Michael got up wordlessly, left the kitchen and went to his mother and father's bedroom. The door was closed. He turned the knob delicately and pushed the door open scarcely wide enough to see the corner of the bed. The room was dark yet he had no difficulty making out the small form of his mother's body as she slept. He closed the door again behind himself and tiptoed back to the kitchen. His father sat glumly, his head in his hands, the tea untouched. "She's sleeping," Michael said.

Taft looked up.

"Mom's sleeping, Dad. You must have been dreaming."

Taft shook his head no. Michael sipped his tea. It was black tea from Ceylon.

"No," said Taft. "I saw her. It was real, real."

"Dad, I saw Mom lying in bed."

Taft rose unsteadily. "Then she's dead," he said, his voice as thick as an impossible sandwich.

"What the hell are you saying?" Michael backed up angrily. "That's crazy! She's sick, all right. But don't go killing her off already."

"I'm not trying to kill her off."

"Yes, you are. That's exactly what you're doing. You're wishing her dead!" His voice was harsh, his words vituperous. "You can't deal with Mom being ill or maybe you just don't want to be bothered taking care of her, so now you're imagining that she's dead!"

Taft shook the cobwebs that mercilessly inhabited his head. It was a curse of old age. He couldn't imagine why his son hated him so. There had been no marker along the highway to say 'Yes, this is the spot. Step right up, folks. This here marks the spot where father and son fought it out, tooth and nail, hammer and claw, flesh to flesh.'

Somehow, like Death itself, this despising had crept into their lives and by the time Aaron Michael had become a young man Taft found himself completely estranged from his only son. It wasn't a happy memory or a happy condition. If only the dendritous cobwebs could erase those thoughts, he would not begrudge them the other damage that they took with them.

"If you don't believe she's dead," Taft said with a cadence like Doom itself, "then why are you yelling? Why aren't you afraid of waking her?" Pain-filled eyes faced his only son "Why aren't you afraid that she'll hear us arguing?"

Michael froze, the handle of the teacup pinched in his finger. He heard the hum of the refrigerator as it worked through the night and the feeble whir of the analog clock on the stove that marked the time. For the first time in a long time, he felt the urge to cry.

Michael pushed back his chair and the legs moaned over the tile. His cup dropped, spilling tea across the table.

Taft braced himself against the nearest wall in the kitchen as his son ran from the room, a man possessed by pain and fear. In a minute, Taft heard the scream that came from the other room and he clutched the wall as if it would keep him from falling into the Devil's arms.

Because that scream he recognized. It was the scream of a son who discovers his mother dead. It was a scream Taft knew only too well. For it was a superhuman sound which had once found its way out his own throat, many years ago. When he'd discovered his own mother dead.

And the cobwebs could never remove it for all their machinations.

# 13

Marie's body was to be flown back to Michigan for burial. The family plot lay outside St. Clair Shores where her mother, Betty, was buried. Marie would be buried beside her. Her father, Edward, was also buried there and, one day too, Taft would join her in that somber plot of soil.

Michael telephoned his sister, Elizabeth, in Warren, Michigan, after the shock and the tumult subsided some and the ambulance and its crew finished their appointed business.

Michael had never been through so morbid and sickening an experience in his life and that didn't even touch on the heartbreaking sadness of those long hours. Michael thought of the many gravesites he had searched in his so-called professional capacity as an archaeologist. He realized that not once had he even sensed at the grief that might have, must have been suffered by those who buried their dead. He only dug them from the ground and studied them like a geologist studied stones and geosyncline deformations.

Taft sat in the living room speaking to a man with a cabbage-like head and cheeks like corundum. The man was from the coroner's office and insisted on asking questions.

Taft's face was ashen and he felt as if it were he himself who had died. He responded to the stranger in monosyllables.

"Elizabeth?" said Michael. "It's me, Michael."

"Michael? Where are you? Is everything all right?"

Michael took a long, slow pull of air. "I'm at Mother and Father's house. And, Mother's dead, Elizabeth."

Elizabeth cried. Her daughter, Judy, asked her what was wrong. "Nothing," said Elizabeth, the mother, soothingly. She ran a hand down Judy's Mississippi mud-colored pigtail. "It's nearly seven-thirty," she said. "Get going now or you'll be late for school."

Judy kissed her mother and ran off in a bundle of coat and books and lunch pail.

"Sorry," said Elizabeth to her brother. "I didn't want to tell her quite yet. I'll wait until she gets home from school to explain it to her. Oh, god, how am I going to do that?" she fretted. Then she shook herself. Life had to go on. "How's Dad?"

"He's quite upset. I think he's a bit cataleptic. He's been acting bizarrely."

"How do you mean?"

"Well, he thought he saw Mother," illustrated Michael. "Running out of the house and into the garden. He broke down the back door and ran after her. I found him out there looking for her. In his bare feet. She was in bed the whole time," said Michael with a visible shudder. He was barely able to hold back his tears as he remembered discovering his mother dead in her bed.

"How awful," answered Elizabeth. "Did Dad find," she almost said 'the body' but it sounded too harsh, too cold and impersonal, "Mother?"

"No, I did. She died in her sleep in her own bed. That's something."

Elizabeth agreed. "She was in great pain, in spite of the morphine, you know."

"No, I didn't know, at least not before yesterday," said Michael with renewed spite. "Seeing how nobody bothered to tell me she was even ill. Now I get less than twelve hours with her and she's dead. How do you think that feels?" He yelled the words at the telephone as if the physical force of the words would carry in shock waves the length of Florida to Michigan.

"Michael!" shouted back Elizabeth. "Calm down, all right. I'm sorry. No one wanted it to happen this way."

"Yes, but it did," he said, relentless and stubborn in his fury. "It did happen that way and you'd think my own father would have the decency to tell me that his wife, my mother is dying, even if my sisters thought they'd play God and keep me insulated from the news—"

"Mother didn't want us to tell you."

"Even," said Michael loudly overriding Elizabeth's rebuttal, "though I was the one who loved her most?"

"That's a bunch of—"

"More than you or him or any of you. I could have helped her. I could have helped her and been here for her and maybe she'd still be alive and now you've all killed her!" Michael screamed uncontrollably. Tears melted down his swollen, unshaven face like great gobs of oil.

"You don't know what you're talking about, Michael. You think you're so much better than everyone else, like nobody knows anything or can do anything as good as you can. You made Dad feel the same way, like he wasn't good enough. Well, I'm warning you, you leave Dad alone, Michael. You leave Dad alone.

"He and Mother loved one another in a way you'll never know. You don't even know what love like that is like. I don't know if you know what any kind of love is like, you've been alone so long. You leave Dad alone," she repeated fiercely.

"What are you talking about? I haven't done anything to Dad."

"Then stop talking that way about him."

Michael sighed, leaking exasperation. "He should have told me," he said stubbornly.

"Mother died. It's not his fault, Michael. You can't blame him for it."

Michael said nothing.

"I'm coming down there," she said.

"But—"

"I'll be there before dark." Elizabeth hung up the phone just hard enough to show her resolve and vent her fury. An instant later, she sunk to the cold Congoleum floor in the kitchen of her usually happy home and cried long and hard for her mother.

# 14

Michael locked himself in his room. Out the back window he could see his father sitting in the garden, the old fool in his habitat. Mother's garden.

The telephone in the living room rang incessantly. Michael didn't answer it though it drove him crazy. It was Dad's house, let him come inside and answer it himself.

Michael tried to read but gave up when he realized that he had read several pages and couldn't remember any of it. He was attempting to read an article in pre-publication form on recent discoveries at Remojadas, an archaeological site in Veracruz, Mexico. The Remojadas culture was known best for its Smiling Head figurines. In the years before Christ, these artisans were busy crafting stylized clay sculptures, many of which contained built-in whistles and rattles, even ocarinas and flutes capable of giving speech to these magical figures.

Accompanying the article were several photographs (or photocopies thereof). One featured a bust of a smiling woman with fine, thin features. She smiled. She looked a lot like his mother. Perhaps they'd been cut from the same mold.

The telephone rang again. Michael paced in his room. He peeked out the curtain and saw his father hadn't moved. At least the sun had turned now and his dad was safely in the shade. It wasn't healthy for him to be out in that sun all the time.

Michael pivoted. Someone was knocking on the front door now. "Damn," he said out loud. He went to give answer to the annoying banging and gave the telephone a nasty look on his way, hoping it would stop its interminable ringing.

With no peep hole like he had at his apartment, he opened the door to the unknown.

A woman greeted him.

She was young, about Michael's age or younger. Her hair was somewhere between blonde and brown and parts of it couldn't seem to make up their mind which direction to fall or maybe there was some sort of gravitational anomaly playing havoc with her head region.

She wore a modest red skirt and a white blouse with practical shoes. She was quite attractive. So was her son.

"Hi," she said. She held out a slender, long-fingered hand. "I'm Ellen. I live next door, well, two doors down," she explained, indicating with a jab of her head that she lived up the road to the right.

Michael shook her hand. "Hi."

"This is my son, Alexander."

Alexander, fidgeting in her grip, all seventy pounds of him, sporting red sneakers, blue jeans that had suffered much abuse and a too large shirt, said hi. He held a box.

"Hello, Alexander," said Michael. Ellen and her son were staring in the direction of the telephone which rang like the bells of the apocalypse.

"I was just coming to get that," said Michael. "Just a second." He picked up the telephone. "Hello?" he said. "Yes, I'll tell him."

Michael put down the telephone. It had been some man named Benji calling for his father. He'd give him the message later. He went back to his guests at the porch. What did they want?

"We heard about Marie," began Ellen. "And we wanted to express our condolences. We knew her quite well. Alexander was very fond of her. She was always so kind to him, Taft too. They kept an eye on Alexander for me when I was working. So kind," said Ellen, unsure of herself. "Are you her son?"

"Excuse me," said Michael, feeling embarrassed yet he couldn't say why. "Yes. My name is Michael. I only arrived yesterday."

"Oh, how sad," said Ellen. She put the palm of her hand on

Michael's bare arm. "We heard you were coming. Again, I'm so sorry. . ."

Alexander twisted out of her grip and went into the living room. "Alexander!" called his mother with a tone of voice that Alex recognized as one he could safely ignore. It was her yellow safety light voice. Meaning I'm watching you, proceed cautiously. But it was no red light.

"Where's Mr. Hart?" asked the child.

Michael turned. "He's out in the garden."

"I have something for him," explained Alexander holding up his box.

"Would you like to see him? Come on," said Michael. "I'm sure he'll be glad to see you." Alexander nodded and led the way as if it were his own home. Michael and Ellen followed after him.

Albert Einstein swept back a lock of hair from his eye. The wind was from the east. It would be warm today. The streets of Anu were radiant. There, in a privately bound edition of the Papyrus of Ani, in the Book of the Dead, in the Chapter of Not Perishing, lived a crisp photograph of Einstein. The great god Temu produced the gods Shu and Tefnut. The children of Shu were Keb and Nut, who produced Osiris, Set, Nephthys, Isis, Anubis and Horus. I mention Horus last for, though he had the head of a hawk, he always had been something of a muckraker and a gadabout.

Nut had a signed limited edition of the Papyrus of Ani. It spread nearly seventy-five feet in length and boasted color illustrations. It was quite rare. And he was quite proud of it.

Einstein surveyed the streets whose cafes and bistros and penny arcades stood empty in Anu except for the occasional passing of a god. Great towers here of unknown design and purpose climbed to the clouds. Yet, for it all, Einstein preferred the Gothic Cathedral of Ulm, the town on the left bank of the Danube where he had been born and where generations of Einsteins had lived before. The spire of the cathedral rose 530 feet into the sky. Often Einstein wondered how tall it had been in the days before feet had been invented.

Certainly more majestic and definitely taller than the towers of the Liebfrauenkirche in Munich which he could view simultaneously (as the last edition of his newest biography had not yet sold out) and which stood only 320 feet apiece.

Albert Einstein could not see Taft in his wife's (dead wife's) garden. Even if he could have, he was not much use when it came to comforting humans. Though, he confessed, he'd needed plenty of comforting himself, and his second wife, Elsa, had provided it for him admirably until her death.

Too bad he had not let Elsa in on his discovery of the photodimension. He might have managed to impose a photograph of his former wife upon Taft and arrange some comfort for him in his time of need.

Marie had provided that strength for Taft and Taft felt the loss severely though it had only been a dozen hours. He felt like a bee-blossom from which sunlight and even the promise of sunrise had been stolen. Days that in his youth were not long enough suddenly seemed painfully too long. And though Michael and Alex and Ellen presumed him to be lost in thought as they approached from the house, he was not. Taft was lost in non-thought. Taft was lost.

"Dad?" Michael studied his father standing like an unsteady ragweed in Marie's garden.

Taft's eyes slowly registered their presence. He smiled when he saw the boy, Alexander. "Hi hi," he said. "I was checking the garden."

"Hi," replied Alexander softly.

Ellen stepped forward and hugged Taft. "I'm so sorry," she said. "If there's anything we can do—"

Taft shook his head glumly. "No, there's nothing anyone can do." He turned to the child. "How you doing, kiddo?"

"Okay, I guess," replied Ellen's son in subdued undertones.

"Dad, you should sit down. You've been standing out here for hours. You're going to get sick."

Hours, thought Taft? "Sure, sure."

"Let's go back to the house," said Michael. "It's too hot out here."

Taft stared at the house as though it were a demon, part hippopotamus, part crocodile, part lion and part furnished by Sears, Roebuck and Montgomery Wards, waiting for him to enter its baited mouth, like a supernatural angler fish, angling for him. "We could sit in the shade," Taft suggested.

"No, come on, Dad, let's all go inside and get something cold to drink. I'm sure Ellen would like something, wouldn't you?"

"Yes, of course," said Ellen willingly.

"I brought you something." Alexander held up the white cardboard box he'd so carefully tied shut and carried with great care to Mr. Hart's house. He handed the box to Mr. Hart with equally great care.

"He's been so secretive," said Ellen, "Even I don't know what he's got in there. I only hope it doesn't jump out, fly away, or bite someone."

Taft took the box solemnly and untied the tiny knot of kite string. Inside, wrapped in tissue paper sat a key. A simple design with a half-moon shaped hole for a chain. The key was well worn and the name etched in its side had been worn away by the touch of many fingers. There was no rust, though it was quite discolored. He held the key in his fingertips.

"It's a key," said Alexander.

Michael looked at the boy.

Taft looked at the key. He looked at the key as if it belonged to a treasure chest buried deep and lost in North Carolina by Blackbeard himself.

"It goes to a case in our garage," he explained. "There's a concertina inside. It was my grandfather's."

Taft looked at the boy, tears aching to come out though he would not let them.

Alexander shifted uneasily on the spongy ground. "He said it had a lot of old songs inside it. He used to shake it like and say 'I hear one coming now' and then he would grip it right up and play whatever song came out of it. It always sounded good."

The boy looked at Taft. "I-I figured you could do that. The case was too big to carry, so I brought you the key. If you want, you can come over to the house and pick it up later."

Taft put the key in his trousers pocket and shook Alexander's hand. "Thank you," he said. "I bet there are some great, great songs in that concertina. We'll look for them together, together, okay?"

Alex nodded affirmatively.

Ellen turned away to keep from crying. Michael stood, looking dumbfounded.

His father had never played a musical instrument in his life! He didn't believe his dad could shake a tune out of a jukebox let alone a concertina.

# 15

Elizabeth arrived and took charge.

She forced her father to take a bath and insisted Michael dress for dinner. She prepared steamed fresh snap beans, baked potatoes and ham.

"Eat," she commanded father and brother. She sat between them in the dining room, watching over them, keeping them from each other. "Come on, Dad Dad," she cooed, "try the beans."

Taft jabbed one on the end of his fork and twirled the green bean in the air where it hung like a circus performer dangling by nicotine-stained teeth from a rope above the crowds who were not eager to watch him fall, but were only too eager to consider the possibility. That was what made life exciting, the possibility of death. He bit off one end of the bean and chewed sluggishly.

Michael ate precisely what he'd been served and didn't ask for seconds.

Elizabeth brewed a pot of coffee and, since the night was cool, they drank it outside on the redwood picnic table below the kitchen window. Michael and his father sat on the same side, facing the expansive yard.

"I'll be right back." Elizabeth set down her cup. "I'd better phone Martin and the kids." Martin was her husband of twelve years. Martin Shoup. A man she loved dearly. The two of them had produced two wonderful girls, Judy, age 8, and Susan, age 6.

Martin worked for General Motors in Warren, at the General Motors Technical Center near Twelve Mile Road and Van Dyke Avenue. He was an engineer, graduated from the University of Michigan in Ann Arbor, which was incorporated in 1851, the same year that overflowing fields of gold were discovered in central Victoria, Australia. This set off a scurrying and hurrying of money seekers, gawkers, looters and killers, all of whose main motivation or compulsion was the power of greed. Among the new settlers were thousands of Chinese and, because they didn't look like the rest of the gold seekers, there were race riots in the fields where dreams were gold. The Victorian government finally felt itself compelled to put severe restrictions on the immigration of Chinese. And thus began the dream of a white Australia.

Martin went to work for General Motors right out of college. He'd attended a job fair in his senior year and been offered the position then and there by a GM representative.

Elizabeth telephoned her home where Martin picked up the receiver in the den on the second ring. They went over the details of their lives and told each other that they loved one another and fought over who missed who more. Elizabeth said to kiss the girls for her. Martin promised he would. He said goodnight. Martin's dream was slow and steady and sure.

Elizabeth listened at the kitchen door before going back outside. Father and son were not speaking. She lifted herself up as best she could (spiritually) and joined them.

# 16

Marie couldn't understand it. She'd figured out that this street was some kind of a Michigan-Florida hybrid of sorts and yet for all the world (or non-world) it looked a lot like Domremy-La-Pucelle, the birthplace of Joan of Arc. The air appeared hazy, and she knew that her eyesight was not as good as it used to be, but she was pretty sure that off in the distance she could make out Le Bois Chenu on the hill where Joan of Arc reportedly (so the stories go) received her miraculous holy visitation launching a mission of rebellion, a Crusade (crusades do not exist anymore; think of it as a pop star's world tour with all the trimmings, if you must) against the English.

She crept quietly up to the steps of the house she and her family had occupied in Lansing, when her father had taken a civil service job there for a time. To the child, Marie, it had been the biggest metropolis in the world. The brownstone seemed tiny now, almost like a doll's house. She went inside. There was the photograph of Albert Einstein. Had there really been a picture like that in her house when she lived there?

She couldn't remember.

She went up the stairs to her bedroom. She recalled it was on the left. Trembling, she pulled back the pale pink quilt from her childhood bed and stretched out. The quilt was an inch or more thick and probably filled with feathers. It kept her warm. She tried not to think of the birds those feathers had been stolen from and how cold they must be.

Marie had discovered that these beds of hers could transport her anywhere. In her mind that is/was. All she had to do was lie down on any bed in any of the houses that she had ever lived in (on this street lined with houses) and the dreams that she had dreamed when she lived there would all come rushing back like a great tidal wave. With practice, she had learned to sort them out and pick and choose among them. Though sometimes they came randomly, like electrons being spit out of a cyclotron or something.

The first time she'd lain down and been deluged by all her old dreams, she'd been scared nearly witless and become soaked in fear-filled perspiration. She had fled, like a colt in a hard wind, only to find herself overwhelmed with curiosity, compelled to return. She still got nervous now, but it was nervous with anticipation of the dreams to come.

Marie re-experienced every dream she had ever dreamt. If she stayed in a bed long enough, she could not even separate the dreams from the reality after a time. But then, reality had become something of an enigma for Marie as well.

# 17

In the morning, Elizabeth knocked on Michael's door. "Michael?" she said. She heard a grumble. "Breakfast is ready." More grumbling. "Come on," she said. "Five minutes or I come in and get you."

Michael scowled and stared out the window. He was already dressed. Had been for a long time. He'd been awake for hours and yet he'd been unable to get any work done at all. To top it off he'd experienced the strangest night he'd ever encountered.

All night long he had dreamt. But his dreams were not his own. They were his mother's. Or at least they seemed to be. He seemed to be dreaming things as if he were his mother and not himself. Maybe he'd ask Steve Niven about that when he got home. Steve was a psychologist at the University of California, trained at Stanford, who specialized in odd brain phenomena. He'd probably have a theory to explain it. He was a man with a theory for everything.

Michael found Elizabeth alone in the kitchen. "Where's Dad?"

"Still sleeping."

"Oh."

She handed Michael some coffee. He drank on his feet. "This is where we stand," she said, commandingly. She proceeded to lay things out for her brother. "I've telephoned the mortuary and I'll be flying back with the—" she flinched, "—with Mom tomorrow."

Michael nodded.

"You and Father will have to drive."

Michael opened his mouth to speak and his sister cut him off with the swift surety of the executioner. "You and Father will have to drive up. You know how Dad Dad hates to fly. Your boss said to take all the time you need."

"My boss?" Michael thought of Randall Cane back in California and wondered, too, how Alan Rushman, the young graduate student of his was doing. Michael had entrusted the young man with the running of his classes while he was away.

"Yes, Dr. Cane said not to worry. He said that he would speak with Max Wapnack about taking over your classes for you in the interim."

Michael was astounded. Max Wapnack was a professor emeritus, semi-retired. He had been far removed from the day-to-day existence of the department for several years now. How had Randall talked him into teaching undergraduate classes of all things? "When did you speak to Randall? And what about Alan?"

"Last night," Elizabeth answered. "Somebody had to do it. I knew you wouldn't have. Dr. Cane thinks that someone other than Alan should handle things, I mean, now that you'll be gone longer than expected. He thinks this fellow Max'll do it."

She scraped flecks of egg and toast off her plate and washed the dish in the sink. "And" she continued, wiping competent hands on her apron (Marie's apron), "I spoke with Rebecca, also. She sounds sweet. Anyway, she said she'd telephone you later."

Elizabeth looked at Michael half-expecting him to elaborate on this Rebecca. On the telephone she'd seemed inordinately interested in Michael. A woman could tell these things. Yet Michael said nothing.

"So, what's the deal?" said Elizabeth turning on her brother with a knowing smile.

"What deal?"

"With Rebecca."

"She's my secretary, our secretary. Works for the entire department, part receptionist, part file clerk. You know," said Michael, obviously discomfited.

"She said she took you to the airport."

"Oh, yes, that. That was nothing. All part of the job, I suppose."

"Uh-huh," deadpanned Elizabeth. She hung her apron on the wooden hook that Dad Dad had screwed to the wall for Marie. For Marie's apron. "Dad and I have to go into town." She checked the time. "I'd better fetch him."

"I'll drive you," offered Michael.

"No, that's not necessary. Besides," she said rather coyly, "your secretary is going to call you, remember?"

"I can't imagine why," Michael answered dryly. "Oh well, I suppose I can use the time. I can't seem to keep up with all the paperwork incumbent upon my job during the best of times, let alone at difficult times like these."

Elizabeth hugged her brother. "See you later," She woke her father, helped him dress and drove him across town.

Michael sat at the writing desk in his room. But he did not write. His mind had been taken from him and his mother's dreams haunted him.

The knocking at the door drummed like a steady hammering. Michael could imagine the incessant hammering and scraping sounds of the Great Pyramid of Egypt being built and how it must have driven the Pharaoh Khufu's neighbors crazy.

Well, there goes the neighborhood, shouted Fred and Ethel Egyptian, as the hordes of construction workers arrived (all sweating and swearing and greased) to begin work on their neighbor's new tomb. Fred Egyptian had to shut the bedroom windows to cut out the noise. For days and weeks and years and decades, the din continued. And when it was over the great gaudy tit on the desert towered over their humble home and gawkers came from miles around just to gawk at it. Yes, there goes the neighborhood. The zoning codes were simply not up to snuff in good old Egypt.

Michael answered the front door before it was knocked to the ground. It was Ellen, sans Alexander. "It's you."

"Hi," said Ellen. "I hope I'm not disturbing you."

"Well—" The ringing telephone interrupted. Michael looked at Ellen as if it were her fault. "Just a second." Michael held the door open. "I'd better get that. Come on in." His words carried no emotion.

Ellen tiptoed into the house and sat on the edge of the sofa. She watched Michael as he picked up the receiver.

"Hello."

"Hello, Michael?"

"Yes."

"It's me, Rebecca Greenleaf."

"Rebecca?" He'd never been aware of her last name before and it took him a moment to recognize who he was speaking with.

"I wanted to tell you how sorry I am."

"Thank you," Michael said. He glanced at Ellen, discreetly folding the pages of a magazine she'd found on the table beside the sofa.

"I know how hard it is to lose someone," said Rebecca. "I lost my mother when I was twelve. I still get lonely."

Michael cocked his head. "You did?"

"Yes. So," she hesitated, "if you need someone to talk to or anything, well, I just want you to know that I'm here if you need me."

"Thanks," said Michael. "I'll remember that."

"You can even phone me at home."

"Well—"

"Let me give you my number." Rebecca rattled off her number and told Michael that she was home almost always after work.

Michael looked about frantically for a piece of paper and pencil and found nothing. He hated it when people started spitting out facts without giving him time to prepare. "I don't have anything to write with," he said. "I'll try to remember."

"I have something," interjected Ellen. "I'm certain of it." She groped around in her balloon-like purse and removed a tiny rose-colored notebook and a collapsible rose-colored pen.

"Thanks," said Michael offhandedly. Rebecca repeated her telephone number and Michael read it back to her. A few minutes later they hung up.

"A friend?" asked Ellen.

"My secretary."

"It was sweet of her to call. It is her, isn't it? I mean, it could be a man, I suppose," said Ellen rather clumsily.

"It's her," answered Michael.

"Then it was kind of her," said Ellen with emphasis, "to call." Why, oh why, must I be so inept? wondered Ellen silently.

"I suppose," Michael carefully ripped out the sheet of paper containing Rebecca's phone number then returned Ellen's pen and notebook. "Thanks again."

He looked at her expectantly. After all she was the one who'd come knocking at his door.

"Anyway," said Ellen, who'd never done anything like this in her life, "I was wondering if you'd like to do something this afternoon? I mean, it's not good for you to be closed up in the house all day and it is Sunday and all. We could go for a drive or something. The beach even, if you want to go that far?"

Michael felt his ears heating up. "No, thanks," he said quickly. "I appreciate your asking. And it's nice of you to be concerned, but I'm fine, really."

"Are you sure? We could do whatever you like."

"No, don't worry about me. I should try to get some work accomplished."

Ellen hid her disappointment well. "I'd better let you get to it then. But if you change your mind," she said at the door, "you let me know, deal?"

"Deal," agreed Michael.

Ellen strode self-consciously down the footpath and turned on the sidewalk to wave goodbye, but she discovered that Michael had already gone inside and closed the door.

# 18

Ellen exacted her revenge quite by chance while standing out on her front drive drying off her freshly-washed automobile. The car didn't look much better scrubbed than it had dirty. But at least she could say that it was clean. Ellen held the washcloth over the bucket and wrung it out. She planned to wipe the windows dry before the water evaporated and left her facing tough water spots.

Elizabeth and Taft drove by.

Ellen waved, her washcloth like a white flag in her grasp.

"Hi," called Taft.

Elizabeth stopped the car at the curb. "Hello," she said through the open car window. She held out her hand. "I'm Elizabeth Shoup."

"Hello," said Ellen, dropping her rag on the concrete, gray as an elephant's behind, and wiping her damp hand on her loose cerise shirt. "It's a pleasure to meet you. How are you feeling, Taft?"

"Okay, okay," He seemed a bit distracted, more than usual.

"Listen," suggested Ellen on the quick, "how about if you all come over for dinner this evening? It'll do you all," she emphasized the word all, "good to get out of the house. Besides, I'm sure you have your hands full taking care of your men, Elizabeth." She emphasized the word men.

Tiny, invisible, girl-type signals passed between the two women. Taft seemed oblivious to them.

Elizabeth grinned a wide, perfect teeth grin. "You're right, Ellen. They do need a lot of looking after. We'd be happy to, wouldn't we Dad Dad?"

Taft said yes.

"Okay, great," replied Ellen. "I'll see you around six o'clock."

Elizabeth waved goodbye and continued up the street to her father's house.

Ellen bent to retrieve her rag, already considering supper. Oh, she wasn't worried about whether to make yams or Idahos, lima beans or spinach. She was wondering what she should wear.

# 19

Brian Pasternak, sturdy, strong, young and alert was driving in his wife's brown station wagon Sunday morning a smidgen over four years ago when another driver, less sturdy and definitely not alert, driving a Nile-green sedan approached from the left oblique. There was a nitid flash and a crunch. When the sound and light waves subsided so too did Brian Pasternak, crushed by the harmless automobile.

The driver of the sedan, though stunned by a blow of head to steering wheel, recovered. He served three months for manslaughter in a minimum-security prison with widescreen TV, racquetball, and a free library where he could improve himself, and never understood why. After all, it had been an accident, hadn't it?

All that remained in Brooksville of Brian Pasternak were the memories in his wife's heart, the even more anguished memories in his young son's somewhat smaller (in terms of measurable mass) heart and a burnished pine door plaque, with the name Pasternak burned into it, hanging above the doorbell of Ellen and Alex Pasternak's house.

# 20

"Ring the doorbell," urged Elizabeth, nervously pushing down the corners of her skirt.

Michael did as directed.

Taft stood on the steps and gazed at the house from a whole new perspective. Since Marie died everything looked different somehow. It was as if the colors had been washed out of everything including the sky, only a shade, but Taft noticed the difference. He was wearing his good suit. Michael wore his, too.

"Come on in," said Ellen, yanking the door open. "Dinner's nearly ready." She hastily wiped tomato-stained fingers on her heretofore clean white apron and pushed back an errant strand of chestnut hair from her forehead. "Have a seat," she begged.

Ellen Pasternak called down the hallway. "Alex, honey, company's here!"

"Okay!" Alexander set down his book, A History of Trains, and climbed off the bed.

"Hi, Alex Alex," said Taft.

"Hi," said Alex.

"Hello, my name's Elizabeth." Alex shook Elizabeth's hand.

Ellen returned with a cork tray balanced on the palm of her hand. "I hope everyone likes the wine. I have some orange juice for you," she added, giving Alex a tall clear glass. She handed around the tray and then sat down on the burgundy-hued sofa beside Taft. He had been there for her, more than anyone else on the block, when her husband had been killed. She would be there equally for him.

The living room extended barely fifteen feet on a side and four adults and a child just about filled it to maximum capacity. The sofa and two chairs and assorted living room appurtenances took care of the rest of the floor space. A walnut-finished spinet piano squeezed between a low bookcase and a writing table. The curtains matched the sofa and chairs. The house felt clean but not to the point of immaculation. Ellen and her son were not the fussy types.

Alex hovered around the edges of the room. He'd started out sitting on the piano bench but had since moved to the floor, the window and now the kitchen doorway. "You want to see the concertina?"

Taft extended and opened his well-aged and hardened hand. "I brought the key."

"Okay," said Alex. "Come on."

Taft rose and followed the boy through the kitchen and out to the garage.

Alex pulled the handle and the big overhead garage door rattled open. There was so much junk in that room that a car couldn't have squeezed in amongst it if it tried. The fat, corpuscular photons of dusk irradiated the dusty, odor-filled garage with red light.

"It's over here," said Alex, climbing over a stack of books and cardboard boxes and making his way to a footlocker on the back wall, half-shrouded with blankets and an old beige trenchcoat.

Taft circumvented the worst of the obstacles and sidled up alongside Alex.

Taft sensed the wispy trail of a dastardly barghest come to portend his misfortune. He chased off the feeling. Misfortunes had come and gone for him. Let fortunes find others to toy with. Taft held out the key. "You open it," he said softly.

"Okay," whispered Alex. He stuck the key in the thoroughly rusted lock and twisted. The lock sprung open with a coughing sound and Alex handed the key back to Taft. Together they opened the trunk and looked inside.

Taft removed an old photo album and gingerly set it aside, revealing a bundle of letters addressed to a Charles Pasternak and various other personal effects, including one octagonal leather case. It was held shut with a simple linchpin. Alex removed the box from the locker and handed it to Taft.

Taft took it in both hands and inspected the leather. He noted some real craftsmanship there. "Let's take it out into the light where we can get a better look at it."

Together they returned the other items to the trunk and Taft locked it once again. He carried the concertina over to a wooden workbench and opened the case. The concertina appeared to glow. Taft was amazed that it appeared in as good condition as it did.

Taft knew that concertinas generally came in three sizes, tenor, tenor-treble and baritone. This one appeared to be tenor and had a chromatic scale of four octaves. Unlike the accordion, the concertina was octagonal and a button-and-wire mechanism opened the double metal reeds. The one-way leather valve flaps on this one remained surprisingly well-preserved considering how long the concertina might have sat neglected.

He gave the bellows a tug and the double reeds, shocked into motion, whined horribly, or perhaps it was only the way he'd played. Sound waves burst through the walls and into the night.

Alexander Prince perked up his ears. Perked up his ears for he had once played on such a concertina. He remembered the sound of that instrument well. Ah, how the nineteenth century crowds had loved him!

Alexander Prince could play the socks of the concertina, and when he played the overture to Richard Wagner's Tannhauser, he knocked his audience dead.

Alexander Prince was a true virtuoso of the concertina. The great Tchaikovsky himself had written parts for four concertinas in his second Orchestral Suite. But the Tannhauser, that had been Prince's claim to fame. Even now, the tale of the minnesinger, Tannhauser, haunted him. He could hear the sweeping sounds of the concertina vibrating through the music hall as Tannhauser sang of his love of Venus and was banished for his praises.

Alexander Prince visited Venusberg Mountain often now, and strolled each spring in the Valley of the Wartburg, greeting Wolfram, Elisabeth and Tannhauser himself outside the gates of Wartburg Castle, the town of Eisenach, birthplace of Johann Sebastian Bach, dwelling idly below. Louis the Leaper (Landgrave of Thuringia) built Wartburg Castle circa 1075 to 1080 and though it is best remembered in history as the retreat where Martin Luther translated the New Testament into German, it would always be the home of Tannhauser as far as Alexander Prince, world's greatest concertinist, was concerned.

"Sounds great," said Alex.

Taft smiled. "Yeah and I bet there are some great songs in here," he said, earnestly peering into the concertina as if the songs were dice waiting to be thrown from the inside out.

# 21

"When is the funeral?" Ellen whispered to Elizabeth in the kitchen. Taft and Alexander stood in the living room showing the Wheatstone concertina to Michael.

"Thursday next," answered Elizabeth. "Dad and Michael are going to drive up. I'm flying back tomorrow with Mother."

"That's nice," said Ellen. She thought of the bronze casket which had carried her husband away. For one irrational moment she had wanted to scream for the pallbearers to stop and bring him back to her. "My husband, Brian," she said. "That's him in that picture there over the table."

Elizabeth studied the photograph on the wall. Brian Pasternak had been a good-looking man. His smile was broad and genuine. "He's quite handsome."

"Yes," Ellen opened the oven door and prodded the roast. "He was killed some time ago."

"I'm sorry."

"That's all right. It was an accident. It happened a long time ago. I still miss him. But Alex, Alex misses him the most. It hurts when you're a little boy and your father is gone."

Elizabeth nodded. In some ways Michael was a little boy, like Alex. Only this time it was the mother who was gone. Elizabeth knew that Michael would never get over Marie's death. He'd never been good at death, never been good at accepting death. And he was a man who made a living, a science, of studying the dead.

Sounds of shouting jolted Elizabeth from her reverie. The tumult was coming from the living room and it was getting louder. She ran.

"Michael!" Elizabeth shouted. All three boys stopped at

once. "What's going on?"

Michael glared.

Alex looked scared. And Taft stood there, looking confused, discombobulated, and hurt.

"Him!" said Michael angrily. "He thinks he's going to play that thing, going on and on about how beautiful it is and what wonderful music is inside it. He's nuts, that's all. Not to mention the fact that Mother has just died. What right does he have to go on like this?" He turned to his father. "Show a little respect!"

"Michael! You show a little respect yourself!" screamed Elizabeth.

"What's wrong?" asked Alex plaintively. "Mister Hart didn't do anything."

"Come on, Alex, dear. Help me in the kitchen," said Mrs. Pasternak. "Everything is all right. It's only a misunderstanding." Ellen led Alex off the scene of family destruction.

"Michael, you're acting crazy," said Elizabeth, her voice a harsh whisper. "I expect you to act your age, especially in front of a child. You know better than that."

"But it's him," whined Michael. "He's talking nonsense and talking about this stupid concertina." Michael expounded, all the while staring angrily at the instrument that Taft clutched in his hands. "He can't even play the damn thing. We shouldn't even be here."

"Where should we be, Michael? Home? Crying over Mother all day long and all night after?" She stared Michael down. "Dad," she said. "Why don't you go give Ellen a hand in the kitchen."

Taft looked at both of them before silently trodding off.

Elizabeth grabbed Michael's arm, hard. "I warned you," she said. "Behave yourself, for god's sake. We've just lost our mother. Dad has just lost the woman he's loved and spent better than fifty years with, Michael. Have some respect for that. You don't know what he's going through."

"But he's carrying on about some stupid concertina," Michael complained.

"So what? Would you rather he sat at home staring at Mother's picture and cried himself into the ground?"

Michael sighed in exasperation. "No, of course not."

"Then leave him alone. Let him handle it in his own way."

"Yes. All right."

"I'm counting on you," said Elizabeth. "Mother is counting on you too. You know that? You have to drive Dad Dad to Michigan, for the funeral. And you can't be arguing and yelling at him the whole way there."

Michael squeezed his eyes shut. "I know," he said softly. "I don't even know why I get so angry with him."

"Try to see his side of things," said Elizabeth.

"I miss Mother," said Michael sadly.

"We all do."

"But he didn't even let me know she was dying. I could have come sooner, I could have—"

"Michael, stop. Dad Dad did exactly what Mother asked him to do. Now you have to do exactly what Mother would want you to do. Take care of Dad."

Michael frowned and said nothing.

"Michael, I'd drive up with Dad Dad myself if I could. But I've got to get back and help Martin with the girls. He can't take too much time away from his job at the moment. That means you have to accompany Dad. Without attacking him and making him feel worse. Be nice to him. He did his best to raise you and take care of you. Now it's your turn. All right?"

"I said I would." He sounded cowed.

"Michael," said Elizabeth menacingly.

"What? I said I would. I'll be nice to him."

"Fine," answered Elizabeth. "You can start right now by apologizing to him."

Michael sighed, but did as he was told. "Sorry, Dad," said Michael, cornering his father in the kitchen.

Seeing his father like that, in that small, odor-filled kitchen, the light coming through the blinds like that—it was a revelation, of sorts.

This was the first time that Michael had noticed that his father had a profile not unlike a denticulated Mousterian side scraper.

# 22

Michael folded the last of his shirts and placed it neatly back in his suitcase, dirty and wrinkled though it was.

He had little else to pack. Most of his things were soiled and he was not inclined to wash them. Fresh clothes didn't last long in Florida's heat and humidity anyway. Maybe he'd purchase new clothes on the road as he needed them.

He left the suitcase openmouthed on the bureau in case there was anything in it he might need before leaving tomorrow. His sister, Elizabeth, was gone. She had driven her rented car back to Tampa International Airport after running into town once again with Taft. Supposedly, they'd gone off on some mysterious errands of their own. They didn't tell Michael what and he did not bother to try and discover their secret. He figured it did not concern him.

Michael gazed toward the ceiling. At this hour, Elizabeth was well on her way to Detroit with Marie. Taft was in his bedroom at the moment, apparently flaying a live sheep judging from the godawful screeching noises emanating from that direction. Michael had already twice cursed the inventor of the concertina, Sir Charles Wheatstone, for chicanery.

Michael passed through the empty living room and spotted Alex out in the front yard washing his father's car. "Alex, what are you up to?" asked Michael, through the open window.

"Hi," said Alex, timidly. He held a slithering green garden hose in one hand and a sopping wet towel in the other. "Mom thought that the car should be clean before you go. Especially the windows."

Michael cracked a grin. "Well," he said thoughtfully. "You don't have to do that. I could do it. Or take it to the car wash."

"I don't mind," said Alex quickly. "I like to help."

"Hold on," said Michael. "I'll get changed and come give you a hand."

"Okay."

Michael returned to his room and changed into a pair of denim jeans that were two inches too long in the cuff and an old T-shirt that he'd brought along on the trip for just such emergencies. It was the cleanest stuff of the bunch. Besides, he'd learned his lesson. He'd mown the lawn in his dress loafers and couldn't get the grass stains off the soles and sides.

A sketch of Mozart embellished the front of Michael's T-shirt, done in indelible black ink. But Mozart couldn't see a thing. He'd never learned to explore the photodimension, though there are those who claim the composer has extraordinary talents of his own, and swear that it's him playing keyboards on the Beatles' Sergeant Pepper's Lonely Hearts Club Band album.

Of course, this would be an aspect of the phonodimension, and Einstein swears that this is impossible and has a pocket full of theorems to prove it.

"I did that side," said Alex as Michael attacked the far side of the Oldsmobile with a fresh rag and an attitude of determination.

"Right," said Michael. "I'll get the top then."

"Okay," said Alex flatly, apparently not one for long-winded speech.

"So," said Michael, in an effort to be cordial and to make up for fighting in front of the boy the night before, "how's school?"

"Fine," said Alex. "I got three books today. From the Scholastic Book Club. Mom lets me order all I want. She says I can buy as many books as I like, so long as I read them."

Michael paused and wiped his forehead. "That's pretty nice of her."

"Yeah," replied Alex. "I've read some really good books. I read one all about an explorer, I can't remember the name, but it's a true story, about how he goes to the Amazon and gets lost and has to fight off the jungle and the bugs and everything until he can find his way home again."

"Sounds interesting. Some of the work I do takes place in the jungle, you know."

"Really?" asked Alex, wide-eyed.

"Really," said Michael.

"I wish I could go to the jungle. Someday," said Alex thoughtfully.

If there are any left by then, thought Michael; a pessimistic thought he kept to himself.

"Are you coming back?"

"What do you mean, Alex?"

"After you go to Michigan. Are you coming back here?"

"Well," muttered Michael, who hadn't really given the matter much thought, "I suppose I'll have to. I've got to drive Dad back after all. So, yes, I guess I will be back."

"That's good," said Alex matter-of-factly. He wound the garden hose onto its wall mount and wrung the water from his washrag. "The car's done." With the final syllable said, the boy ran off down the street.

Michael stood all alone on the sidewalk. Something was happening to his life, to the insulated little burrow that he'd made for himself, and it scared him.

# 23

Michael groaned when the alarm went off like fuzzy thunder beside his bed. He woke with a headache. Five o'clock in the morning was no time to be getting up; especially when it was two o'clock in the morning in Santa Barbara. He'd never grow accustomed to the time difference.

Still, it had been his idea to get an early start. He hated driving long distances and hated it even more when it was hot and traffic was heavy. He heard his father stirring about the house. He smelled fresh coffee. Didn't the man ever sleep?

Michael showered, shaved and dressed casually for the trip. This included a pair of sneakers, and he nearly tripped trying to figure out how to walk without a standard heeled shoe. In town he strictly wore dress shoes. Out in the field, he wore boots. Lots of the graduate students ran around everywhere in sneakers, but not Michael. He'd owned the same pair of sneakers since college and they still had years of tread life left on their soles. Even the shoelaces looked brand new.

"Morning, Dad," he said as he crept into the kitchen. Prowling on sneakers, he felt as if he should be dribbling a basketball. It was the reason he'd bought them in the first place. He'd thought then that he might play some basketball for recreational purposes. His college roommate at the time had talked him into playing the game. "Try a sport," he'd said. Michael tried it once and gave up. Too much running around for nothing.

"Coffee's ready," said Taft.

Michael poured himself a cup.

"Want some breakfast?"

"No," answered Michael sleepily. "It's too early. I'll wait

till we stop." Michael dribbled an imaginary basketball with his fingertips.

"Okay."

"How about you?" Michael turned.

"I ate some toast," said Taft, eyeing his son curiously.

"I suppose I should start loading the car." He shot. Two points. Or was it three?

"Already done."

"Everything?" Michael blew a puff of air across the surface of his coffee.

"Except for your stuff. I didn't want to disturb you."

"Okay, I'll get my things together and we can go."

Taft nodded his head in accord. He listened to the sounds of Michael busying himself in the other room. They were good sounds, clicks and scrapes and throat clearings. Feet walking. Water taps tapping. Lungs breathing, hearts beating beating. Those sounds reminded him of all those growing up sounds he used to hear in the house; with a wife, three girls and a son there were plenty of sounds all the time; day and night, night and day. And times in between that he never knew existed.

He was going to miss sounds. He missed the sounds that his children made. He would miss the sounds that Marie would make. The little sounds that made him feel better, more secure, just knowing she was there.

Taft was grateful that he'd been there for her in her time of need, but still, sometimes, he wished—just a tiny wish—that he'd have died first and been spared the being left behind.

He rinsed the two coffee cups in the sink and dried them meticulously with a thick white towel. The dish towel featured a picture of a large asparagus with a description and growing tips. *The calcium and phosphorus rich plant grows best in temperate zones. Beds should be of sandy loam or loose, well-drained clay. A good asparagus bed could produce for fifty years.*

Taft set the clean cups back in the cupboard and checked the back door and all the windows to see that everything was locked up. He didn't want anything getting in or out.

Taft waited for Michael out on the porch.

"Ready?" asked Michael. He'd loaded his suitcase and briefcase.

"Yes," answered Taft. He took a long look at the house and turned the key in the lock.

They stopped the car in front of Ellen and Alex's house and Michael knocked on the door.

"Hi," said Ellen, bleary eyed but alert, "Come on in for a minute."

Michael and Taft stood in the entryway.

"Don't worry about the noise," she explained. "Alex is already up."

Alex appeared as if cued. "Good morning."

Taft and Michael said hello.

"Here are the keys," said Taft, handing Ellen a set of house keys.

Ellen took the keys and set them on the piano. "Don't worry, I'll take good care of the place."

"What about me?" demanded Alex.

"*We'll* take good care of the place," she said giving her son a playful headlock.

"We'd better go," said Michael.

"Right," said Taft.

"Wait, just a minute," said Ellen. She ran to the kitchen and came back with a cooler and a stainless-steel Thermos bottle. "I thought you could use these for the trip." Ellen handed the supplies to Michael who accepted them awkwardly.

"There's some sandwiches and stuff and coffee in the Thermos." She brushed back her hair and picked up a map from the table. "This too," she said. "It's a map of the United States. I didn't know if you had one." She looked at Taft and Michael with uncertainty.

"No," replied Michael, quite surprised at her thoughtfulness and his own lack of foresight. He hadn't even thought to take a map.

His father nudged him. "Tell her thank you."

"Thank you," Michael said, uncomfortably and without daring to make eye contact. He wasn't good at accepting things.

He carried the cooler chest to the car and set it on the backseat. Taft carried the coffee and the map. Taft hugged Ellen and shook Alex's hand. "See you soon soon."

"Bye," said Alex. The boy noticed the concertina on the front seat and smiled.

"Yes, goodbye," said Michael awkwardly.

Ellen extended her arms and gave Michael a tender embrace. "Take care of each other," she said. "And don't worry about the house."

Ellen and her son stood on the sidewalk and waved to Taft and Michael as the car disappeared down the hill and around the corner.

Back at Taft's house, a tiny Calliope hummingbird flew forward and then backwards over Marie's wide garden. With its bright green back and crown it appeared like a flying emerald. Her white chin and the pale salmon-colored wash on her flanks identified her easily as a female.

In that same instant an oilbird, the guacharo (Steatornis and relative of the goatsucker) returned from a night of feasting (he preferred palm nuts to codling moths) on the Isla de Margarita to his home in the caverns near the seaport of Cumana, Venezuela. A wonderful natural harbor provided shelter and the sea was splendid. His cavern was cool and he shared it with a hundred feathery friends. And though the natives here had a nasty habit of boiling the guacharo young for household fat and butter substitute, location, as they say in the real estate business, was everything.

"Do you know where we're going?"

Michael shrugged without taking his hands off the steering wheel. "I guess so. North."

Taft laughed. "We need to get the interstate," he said.

"Which way should I go then?"

"Take a right on Highway Ninety-eight. That'll take us to the interstate. I-Seventy-five. Then," said Taft with emphasis, "we go north."

"How far do we have to go, anyway?"

"You mean to Detroit?"

Michael nodded, eyes glancing off road markers, road lines and passing cars.

Taft considered. "Well, well," he drawled. "Marie and I used to make this trip a couple of times a year, you know. And I'm still not sure of the mileage. I was never one for counting the miles. Near as I can guess, it would be about twelve hundred miles."

"That doesn't sound so bad."

"It shouldn't be," agreed Taft. "Not this time of year. It'd be worse if we were going in January or something, the dead of winter. Snow on the highways, in the mountains."

"Sounds pretty."

"It is."

Michael turned onto Interstate 75 and aimed north. Soon the car and its passengers were lost in a hypnotic voyage.

A couple of hours out they stopped at a rest area replete with picnic benches and restrooms. They drank Ellen's coffee and scavenged the cooler for sweets. They saved the sandwiches (ham and turkey) for lunch. Taft went to the bathroom and popped a couple of pills. He studied himself in the polished steel-framed mirror. It wasn't a pretty sight.

In the early afternoon they arrived in Macon, county seat of Bibb County, Georgia (so named for the largest employer in the area, the Bibb Company) and Michael suggested they stop. In spite of frequent breaks for car and body refueling and leg stretching and rear end airing, he was worn out from being locked in the driving position and his backside was sore from sitting all day.

"Okay," agreed Taft. He was feeling none too well himself. The constant motion of the automobile was upsetting his stomach.

Michael and Taft agreed on the Wilson Motor Lodge located off College Street near the downtown historic district. It was small and clean. The L-shaped motel was typical Georgia colonial style, painted white with a white tile roof and shutters of green.

The office was in the front. The desk clerk, with her dark hair drawn primly back from her fleshy face, was matronly. Her accent was thick as unrefined maple sap. Michael went in and registered while Taft sifted through the bank of brochures lining the wall next to the window. He removed several.

They carried their bags to their room and, unspoken, they each sat on the beds and groaned with satisfaction. The air conditioner was already running.

Taft read his brochures. "Look." He pointed. "Says here that there's an important archaeological site right in Macon."

Michael looked at his father. Sometimes he didn't think his father even knew what he did for a living and now the man was talking archaeology? What next, he'd discover that his father had been a charter subscriber to American Anthropologist?

Taft continued speaking. "The Ocmulgee National Monument," he read, "They say here that it represents the remains of some Indians called Mound Builders and dates back as far as eight thousand BC."

"I'm familiar with it," said Michael lazily. "Creek, I believe.

"We could go, if you like."

"I don't know."

"I wouldn't mind seeing it myself."

"I wouldn't mind either. I just hate getting back in the car."

"We'll go tomorrow," said Taft, cheerfully, happy to be sharing something with his son besides rancor. "We can go there first thing and then get on the road afterward," Taft continued enthusiastically. He spoke without looking at his son, as if afraid of the answer, the objections, all the reasons why they shouldn't go.

"Okay," said Michael. "It might be fun." He shut his eyes.

Taft couldn't help smiling. "Think I'll wash up up." He went into the freshly-sanitized bathroom and shut the door.

Taft opened both water taps, hot and cold, as far as they would go. Water splashed noisily against the basin and splashed up the sides. Satisfied, he lifted the lid on the toilet, bent to his knees and vomited into the clean white bowl as quietly as he could manage.

# 24

They spent the better part of the morning exploring the fortifications, ceremonial mounds and burial mounds of peoples long dead. Michael explained the fine art of excavation to his father who listened attentively. Though the presence of death burned his nostrils. Vibrissae recoiled and turbinated bones shook his cranium. He could be walking on the very dust of the dead.

Unlike most people, Taft held a firm belief in death. Perhaps that was why the thought of it shook him so much. And like the Pelagians, he did not believe in the Original Sin. If there had been an Adam and he fucked up, it was only himself that he'd screwed. There had to be some free will in the world. Somebody had to create all that dust.

They opened up the car doors to let the hot humid air out and the cooler humid air in. Taft slapped the dust from his trousers and climbed behind the wheel. "I'll drive," he offered.

"Are you sure?"

Taft nodded. "Give me the keys." He held out his palm. Michael gave his father the car keys and made room for himself on the passenger's side. He set the concertina on the floor between his feet.

Taft rather deftly managed to locate the interstate and he maintained a steady sixty miles per hour. Navigating around Atlanta was hell and, once they were safely out of the city, Taft turned the wheel over to his son. "I think I'll try to sleep," he said weakly.

Michael drove while his father tilted back his seat and shut his eyes. Everything was fine for about ten minutes. But he couldn't hold it. Taft vomited all over himself, the front seat, and the floor.

"Jesuschrist," said Michael, swerving in shock. "What's going on? Are you all right?"

Taft doubled over and coughed between his knees. He was shaking and sweat broke out on his face, neck and arms. "I'm all right," he managed to spit out between heaves.

"Hold on," said Michael. "I saw a sign for an exit coming up in a couple of miles."

Taft nodded and took deep breaths.

"You can get cleaned up then."

Michael took the exit and headed for the closest gas station. The one he found looked like it had been built in the forties, and most recently updated in the fifties. He pulled up next to the garage bay and helped his father out of the car. The smell of grease and gasoline permeated the air. The gas pumps were vintage World War II, the prices contemporary.

"Can I help you?" asked the mechanic, eyeing the filth-covered old man and his companion with suspicion.

"It's my father," said Michael, himself considering that the term 'grease monkey' suited this particular denizen well, "he's not feeling well. Can we use your restroom?"

"Sure," said the mechanic. "I'll getcha the key." He ambled over to an oil-and-bug residued wall and returned with a key on a stick of wood the size of a little league baseball bat. "Here y'go."

"Thanks," said Michael. "You all right now?" he asked his father. Taft nodded. "Okay, get cleaned up then. I'll fill up the tank while we're here."

Taft went to the restroom and washed off his face and arms. When he got back to the car, he pulled a fresh shirt out of his suitcase and changed in the men's room. He balled up the soiled shirt and dropped it in the trash bin behind the service station. No point carrying the stinking thing in the car all day. By the time he returned, Michael had already gassed up the car and was sipping a soda.

Michael asked, "You want anything?"

"No."

"You sure? It'll do you good, Dad. You didn't eat a thing this morning and you barely ate at all last night. No wonder you threw up. You've got to eat something."

"No, thanks," said Taft. "I'm really not hungry."

"Then have something to drink."

"I had some water," lied Taft. Well, he had rinsed his mouth out in the sink.

"Okay," Michael shook his head, "suit yourself. But if you get sick again don't blame me."

"I won't," agreed Taft.

They spent the night in London, Kentucky.

The Daniel Boone National Forest was a presence that hung over them like a cloud of pine trees and evergreens, beech and walnut, ash and linden intermingled with fields of goldenrod.

Gray squirrels and possums and woodchucks helped to provide the noises that made the forest real. Lying in his narrow bed, Taft heard them all. He smelled them and, if he tried hard enough, he believed he could even talk to them or, at least, share a deeply profound feeling with them all. He dreamt that he was sleeping in the middle of that black forest, safely in Nature's arms.

# 25

Michigan came on like a dream remembered. The interstate cut right through the city and right past Tiger Stadium. Taft and even Michael could remember a time when it did not.

Nathaniel Hart, fingers a blur of musical motion as hands swept over the Todeschini accordion and smoke curled through the beer garden, pricked up his ears. Somewhere, he knew that his son and his grandson were walking those streets of his. He played faster and louder.

"I can't believe how much everything has changed," remarked Michael. It had been ages since he'd been in Detroit. Except for Elizabeth, he had not seen his sisters in an equally long time.

Taft only nodded.

"Wasn't our house along here somewhere, Dad?" Michael steered the car onto Interstate 696 at Taft's instruction.

"We had a house when you were born born out this way," said his father. "They tore down part of Eleven Mile Road and put up the interstate later. That's why you don't recognize it."

"Right," said Michael. "I forgot. My kindergarten school was on Eleven Mile Road. Now it's a freeway."

"You can exit at Van Dyke," said Taft.

"Okay." Michael watched the signs and gazed off the highway to the city that bulged up around it. Though he'd grown up and spent a fair part of his life there, he couldn't think of anyone from those days that he was still friends with. Michael had never been one for friends.

Michael got in the far right lane and followed his father's directions to Elizabeth and Martin's house. They passed the

General Motors Technical Center on the way.

If Michael remembered correctly, his father and mother used to take him and his sisters to a big show that General Motors put on every year in the area. The company had a tank plant or something and each year they put on a big outdoor show for the locals. Tanks rolling over cars as easily as a man stepping on a June bug. Parachutes hooked up to ropes hanging from high poles and you could jump off of them like a real paratrooper might.

Michael wondered if those shows still existed. He'd have to ask Martin and Elizabeth. His father did not seem to know. Surely, General Motors would still have a tank plant. The need for engines of war never seemed to diminish.

The first armored track laying vehicles, forty-nine in number (shipped in secret in crates labeled Tanks, hence the name) saw battle duty during World War I. The British employed them at the Battle of the Somme near Courcelette, in France, on September 15, 1916. "The falling leaves fall and pile up; the rain beats on the rain." So said Gyodai, the haiku poet.

Michael felt he was right. The British hadn't fared well that day. The German Army was well emplaced. Michael often considered the possibility that all of humanity was mad. Perhaps it was a genetic flaw or mishap. Maybe humanity was a splinter group sent here by its mother civilization because of its madness. A sort of leper colony for a race of lunatics.

Arriving at the house, Elizabeth's oldest daughter, Judy, was playing in the front yard. She was wearing a long sleeve pink blouse and a tartan wool skirt. Her face was round and soft, like her mother's. She'd traced a hopscotch board on the sidewalk leading to the front door with a stick of chalk and was using a flattish rock for a marker.

Michael pulled into the driveway slowly, always frightened that any child might react in a bizarre fashion and do something completely crazed, like jump in front of a moving car, like the one he was behind the wheel of.

Michael wasn't used to children.

Judy stopped her game and stared. Taft waved at his grandchild. Judy dropped her rock and ran to greet him. "Grandpa!" She squealed with delight.

"Hi, hi, little girl," said Taft, lifting Judy off her feet and squeezing her like a doll.

"Mommy's in the house," she said, "With Christie." Christie was her three-year-old younger sister.

"Hi," said Michael.

"Hi, Uncle Michael," said Judy, shyly. He was nearly a stranger to her. "Are you going to stay with us? Mom said you would."

"Yes, I suppose we will," said Grandfather Taft. "That is, if you'd like us to?"

"Yeah, yeah," said Judy. She ran toward the house. "Mommy! Grandpa and Uncle Michael are here!" The storm door slammed behind her.

Elizabeth, in a black wool sweater and blue jeans tucked into tan leather boots stuck her head out the side door near the driveway. "Hi. How was the trip?"

"Fine," said Taft.

"We thought you'd be here earlier."

"We took our time," said her father. "And we stopped to look at some Indian ruins. Ocmulgee National Monument."

"Oh?" Elizabeth looked at her brother for an explanation.

Michael caught her gaze. "It wasn't my idea," he said in self-defense. "Dad wanted to go."

"Right, right," said Taft.

"Come on in the house. It's about fifty degrees out here and, Dad, I know you're not used to that anymore."

"Bah, feels good," said Taft, rubbing his hands with relish. "I miss it."

"You won't miss it come January and Martin and the neighbors are out here trying to shovel a path down our street for the cars to get out."

Taft laughed. "No, I guess I wouldn't miss that. Though I don't have such bad recollections of those times," he added. "Do you kids remember that winter in the first house when the wind sent those snow drifts right up to the eave of the roof?"

Michael and Elizabeth both said they remembered.

"Couldn't even get the doors open," recollected Taft.

"I remember," said Michael. "When the wind died down and you were able to force the back door open, you and Mother let us kids out to play. I got my coat stuck on the fence on the side of the yard. I thought I was going to sink up to my ears in the snow before Elizabeth and Mary pulled me off."

Inside, the kitchen was warm and moist. Taft bent over and held his cold, stiff hands over the floor radiator vent. "Just like the old days," he said.

"I'll make some coffee," said Elizabeth. "Why don't you bring the luggage in before it gets dark."

"Okay," said Michael.

"Judy, why don't you give Uncle Michael a hand."

"All right, come on, Uncle Michael, I'll race you." She took off in a burst of juvenile energy. Michael, all reserve and no impulse, followed steadily behind.

"Well?" demanded Elizabeth. She gave her father a hug.

"Well what?"

"How are you?"

"Fine, fine," said Taft. "Nothing to worry about."

"I made an appointment for you first thing tomorrow morning."

"But Elizabeth—"

"But nothing, Dad Dad. You know," she said with stern emphasis, "that you have to."

"Yes," said her father meekly.

"Go," said Elizabeth, giving her father a gentle push. "Read the newspaper while I fix the coffee. And say hello to your granddaughter, Christie. She's in there watching Sesame Street. She can't get enough of that program."

Taft found the day's copy of the Detroit News on the sofa. Christie was sitting several feet from the television, dressed in a yellow-and-red one-piece flannel pajama. "Hello, Christie."

Christie turned around. She had milky white skin and fine blonde hair. "Hi," she said with timidity.

"Remember me?"

"You're Grandpa," she said.

"That's right," said Taft happily. "So, so, how's about giving Grandpa a kiss and a hug?"

Christie goose-walked over to her grandfather and they embraced.

"It's good to see you," said Taft. Christie sat on the floor, her back against the sofa, beside her grandfather. She watched the television as he read the newspaper.

The printed word used to have such value and now it was thrown away at the end of the day. Trash for the landfills or recycled for more newsprint. In Christopher Plantin's time (c. 1520-1589) the written word was inviolate. Something to be cherished and preserved. The patrician building where he ran his printing press in Antwerp near the Grand Place, at Vrijdagmarkt 22, still exists. For over three centuries it served its function until being converted to a beautiful museum. Rubens and Van Dyke once walked its halls and its rooms are filled still with priceless manuscripts and first editions.

And outside you can purchase Le Monde and any one of a dozen other newspapers and paperback books and the overflow ends up in the trash. Plantin's motto had been "Labore et constantia."

Besides the Polyglot Bible and hundreds of other editions, he'd been responsible for the publication of the works of many of the leading botanists of his time, including de l'Ecluse, Dodoens and Lobel.

Plantin was, as a printer, particularly proud of the job his shop had done on Dodoens' "Stirpium historiae pemptades ex sives libri XXX," first printed in 1583 and reprinted after the death of its author and Plantin himself.

Plantin had consulted it often himself whenever he was unsure of a plant's distribution or characteristics.

It was the kind of book Marie would have liked.

# 26

Martin, red hair and freckles, and a stiff crew cut head of hair that looked like it was held up in front with shellac, came bounding into the living room.

"Martin," admonished Elizabeth, "why didn't you come in through the kitchen?"

Martin looked at his guilty muddy shoes. "Sorry," he said with a childlike grin.

Elizabeth shook her head. "You could at least try to stay on the footpath. Here, give those shoes to me."

Martin leaned one arm against the living room wall and untied his shoes. He handed them gingerly, by damp brown shoelaces, to his wife.

"I'd set them on the back stoop," she said, "but they'd probably freeze in the night." Instead, she arranged them on a piece of newspaper by the kitchen door.

"Hello, Taft. Hello, Michael," said Martin to the two men who'd witnessed his ignominious entrance. "How was your trip?"

"Not bad," said Michael.

"Daddy," said Christie, "Grandpa watched Sesame Street with me."

"That's nice," answered Martin, picking up his daughter and swinging her chest high. "How are you, Dad?"

"Can't complain," answered Taft. "How about you? How's life at General Motors?"

"Busy. Profitable. Not in a monetary sense, mind you," Martin added quickly. "I mean that the job keeps me interested—mostly."

"That's more than many can say," Taft replied. He

understood the value of that in a man's life.

"What are you working on?" asked Michael, feeling such questions were socially obligatory.

"Trying to figure out how to drop fifty-seven pounds from a prototype car the design team's dreamed up. Not as easy as it sounds," Martin replied, settling his socked feet down on the footstool and leaning back in the easy chair that he still had five payments on as part of a living room shopping binge he and his wife had gone on nearly seven months ago.

They'd bought a new sofa, three chairs of various sizes (like the Three Bears), two end tables, a coffee table, three lamps and a combination stereo/television center in a walnut cabinet. And one footstool (now in use). "Can't simply knock out the backseats or leave out the spare tire—"

According to Boyle's Law, the volume of a given mass of gas held at constant temperature is inversely proportional to the pressure under which it is measured. Taft Hart, resting on the sofa, right arm clutching a lumpy cushion, observed an example of this law at that very moment. The experiment was taking place in his bowels. And he was not a comfortable observer. He was not even an objective observationist. "Excuse me," he said, twisting out of the sofa. "I have to go to the bathroom."

Taft fled the living room as fast as he could manage without losing his dignity. He ran to the bathroom down the hall and to his right. He closed and locked the door behind him. He turned on the hot and cold water taps full blast and pushed open the tiny bathroom window all the way. Cold Michigan air mixed with his internal gases.

Taft gasped and tottered over the sink, overcome with the dry heaves. He splashed his face with water and dried himself off. He felt a line of sweat accumulating along the back of his neck.

Taft then turned off the water and shut the window. The room had turned cold. Frigid air seemed trapped in the ceramic tiles of both walls and floor. The tiles were custard yellow and just the sight of them made Taft want to puke. His guts obliged and he spilled black fluid over the floor before managing to lift the toilet seat with both hands and vomit some more.

When his traitorous body was done, Taft rose. Defeated and ashamed. Embarrassed, though there was no one there to see his loss. He removed the roll of toilet paper from the chrome holder and peeled off layer after layer. Taft used the toilet paper to clean up the floor and wipe off his shoes. He carefully wiped the rim of the toilet bowl clean and flushed everything down.

Taft rinsed and gargled and spit fiercely into the custard yellow sink. Robert Boyle, of Boyle's Law fame (unless you're talking to Edme Mariotte, the French physicist who was born seven years before Robert Boyle and died an equal number of years before Boyle's death and who likewise liked to spend his time studying the significance of gases and constant temperatures and such and who likes to think of that same Boyle's Law as Mariotte's Law) wrote a tome entitled "Discourse of Things Above Reason."

And though Taft had never read that particular book, he knew that it must be a big one.

# 27

The next day they buried Marie's earthly remains. It was raining. The sky was battleship grey and the rain took on a steady-state flow. The Grand Haven Cemetery stood empty except for their small funeral party. A row of dark cars lined the cul-de-sac and everyone slowly gathered round the hole in the ground where Marie would lie for all eternity.

Michael rode in the third car and got out, unmindful of the rain that soaked through his best suit. He wore no overcoat. His breath came out in clouds and he plodded on heavily through the wet grass.

The wind blew in from the lake and the trees swayed like stands of mourners weeping mournfully. Cemetery staff erected a canvas tent to keep out the rain over the family plot. The flowers that wouldn't fit under the tent with the family were covered with sheets of plastic. As if it mattered.

Michael studied his sisters. They were all there, as one. The entire clan was there. They never managed to get together in life but one good death and they all gathered. Elizabeth, Mary and Cora. He used to call them the Gorgon sisters. Like Stheno, Euryale and Medusa, the three brooding daughters of Phorcys and Ceto.

And though it was not the most flattering of comparisons (since the Gorgon sisters were horrible to gaze upon with their dragonlike bodies and huge wings with ugly pug faces and ran about with their tongues hanging out) it was, nonetheless, an image that Michael often teased his three older sisters with.

And Cora, Cora could only have been Medusa, the only one of the threesome who could have been killed. She'd always seemed the most vulnerable of them all. She cried now, though it would be hard to say that her tears were any more painful than those of the others.

None of them looked so immortal standing there today, leaning over that hole in the rain. It took no Perseus to destroy them, only the slow march of time.

Michael took his place beside the coffin and watched stiffly as the shiny box was placed in the ground. Edward and Betty, her dear departed parents, sighed and rolled over, making room for their daughter. The straps were released and the cleric whispered some quiet words of hope and profundity.

Michael couldn't hear the man's words, they seemed to swim past him like a salmon struggling in mud. The fulcrum of his life had been set six feet under never to rise again. Soon the swift, sharp blade of the spade would bury his mother's bones forever. Almost in reverse fashion as the manner in which Michael spent his life digging up the bones of other mothers, though he used finer instruments, a toothbrush and a dental pick.

He saw aunts and uncles and relatives whose names and faces he could not recall. He plucked a flower from a bouquet of roses and dropped it onto the coffin. There came a momentaneous shiver of the ether as if someone was shaking a plastic sheet across the air, distorting the background.

Michael gazed down at the rose that had settled atop the casket and thought thoughts too private to share.

Taft shuddered. He stood near the edge of the canvas, his back soaked from the rain that caught at him. He said nothing. After all, they'd just cut out his heart and buried it there in the mud. What could a man say?

Beneath the great sala trees whose branches were never free of leaves even in winter, the Great One lay dying. The Tathagata. The Perfect One. The Buddha. With a belly like that of a year-old baby. It was December (Margasirsa). The town of Kusinagari lurked nearby and the river Hirajnavati carved its path through the woods as if it would carve the face of a jack o' lantern on the faceless earth.

Buddha was eighty years old and though he died thousands of years before Marie, he had outlived her by many years. "Now then, o Monks, I remind you," he said. "Subject to decay are all composite things. Strive diligently for liberation."

These were his last (mortal?) words.

# 28

Cora held the wake at her house. Cora and her husband Troy lived in Rochester, an enclave of the well-to-do. They looked more like brother and sister than husband and wife. Cora's short black hair looked almost mannish. Troy had the same hair and soft, delicate features which made him look almost womanish. And when they got all cute and wore similar outfits, they looked for all the world like an oddball experiment gone awry.

Cora and Troy Jensen made mortgage payments on a fine, sprawling home with a tile roof, a fifteen-meter heated swimming pool and jacuzzi on a rise of land in the center of their upper-crust community. It wasn't a mansion by any stretch of mind but it was more than anyone needed. The master suite was as large as Michael's entire residence.

Troy was an architect and had taken the existing home and remodeled it when he and Cora married. She did the interior decoration though she'd had no previous experience. You don't need a piece of paper to say you can do something, you just have to want to do it.

Cora got the job done. They'd occupied the home for better than five years now but this was the first time Michael had set foot inside. He wiped his shoes carefully before braving the white carpeting that stretched out over the living room floor daring somebody to set foot on it. The rain had enveloped Rochester as well.

Most of the funeral party had already arrived. Others here now, too. Friends who hadn't been at the funeral service but came for refreshments afterwards. A cast copy of Constantin Brancusi's 'The Kiss' stood on a pedestal opposite the flagstone fireplace. The fire itself seemed the most alive thing in the room. Maybe it was only that it consumed oxygen at a greater rate than any person in the room.

Michael poured himself a glass of wine and stood off by himself in one corner. Taft hid in the kitchen with Cora and Elizabeth. They were busy preparing food for the guests who had come to honor their mother. Taft's wife. Mary, the middle born, performed the duty of hostess in Cora's absence.

"You all right, Dad?" asked Cora. Her father leaned weakly against the kitchen table. The southern pine was nearly her father's age.

"Yes," said Elizabeth. "You should sit down Dad Dad." It was a day that had to be gotten through. Holding a cheese knife in one hand, she arranged crackers and cheeses around a teak serving tray with a centerpiece of daffodils. Her hair was tied up with a black ribbon.

Taft felt as if he'd swallowed ten Narcissus bulbs. He slid a chair out from the table and sat. Cora came and held his hand. Only one small oily tear escaped from his lacrimal gland. Maybe his lacrimal gland was rusty. Or defective.

Taft had never seen his own father, Nathaniel, cry. But that day, in the beer garden on Lafayette Street, Nathaniel's accordion cried buckets full.

"How about some coffee?" offered Elizabeth.

Taft nodded.

Elizabeth handed him a cupful with a bracing splash of Napoleon brandy. He sipped slowly. "Do you want to stay here, Dad Dad, or would you like to join everyone in the living room?"

"I think I'll just sit sit here for a time."

"Okay," said Elizabeth softly. "I'd better go see how things are going and take some food out." She picked up the serving platter in one hand and grabbed a bottle of white wine in the other.

"I'll stay here, too." Cora did not want to leave her father unaccompanied.

"Go ahead," replied her father. "It's your house, you should be out there."

Cora only held her father's hand all the harder. She followed his gaze out the big sliding glass doors. The pool was covered now to keep the leaves and debris from falling in. And the glass doors were sealed shut to keep the leaves and debris from flying inside and joining them in the house. Leaves and debris don't have many options in the winter time. Seems nobody wants them at all.

The grass was brown. The sky gray. The rain (as someone once said) beat upon the rain.

For a second, Taft forgot about death. Forgot that he'd left his wife lying in a hole near a lake. Forgot that he'd been left behind to walk on the surface of the earth (like a fly beating against the glass) as if he had yet to achieve a higher level. A level that would allow him to shake off his mortal body and penetrate to another level.

At that moment, he wished that he'd brought the concertina with him. He felt suddenly like playing. The moments ticked by in his head.

# 29

"How's Dad?" asked Martin.

Elizabeth shrugged and looked around the room. There must have been fifty people here. Judy and Christie sat on a sofa quietly sipping sodas. "Okay, I guess." She gave Martin an unexpected kiss. "He'll come out when he's ready."

"Help me open the wine."

Michael wandered down the hall to one of the guest rooms. The door stood open and coats piled atop one another on the bed. He moved a heap of them to one side and stretched out beside them. He felt a million years old. Someone could pick over him right now with a trowel. Louis Leakey take my bones, he thought.

He jumped hearing the noise coming from the bathroom located in the rear of the bedroom. It sounded like someone was kicking a dying mule who had swallowed a carburetor and was trying desperately to reverse the process. But peristalsis is a stubborn mechanism. Michael didn't know whether to make a graceful exit or see if he could be of assistance. It was Cora's house, perhaps he should seek her out and let her deal with it?

The sounds of upheaval became louder and all the guest coats in the world wouldn't muffle it. In the end, he decided he'd better knock. Hesitantly, he tapped at the bathroom door. Tap tap. "Hello. Are you all right in there?"

Michael held his breath, listening. Nothing. Maybe a low groan. "I mean, I was coming by and couldn't help but hear."

"Hello?" He listened again. Nothing again. "I know it's embarrassing and all. If you're all right—"

Definitely a low groan. A sigh. Or a leaky toilet. The hard tile surface reflected and distorted the sounds coming out from behind the door. He resisted the temptation to try the handle. The last thing in the world he was in the mood for was to see some fellow sitting on the toilet with his pants around his ankles conducting his business.

"Hello?" Michael was getting annoyed now. He knocked louder. A sudden wave of carburetor-mule-kicking convulsions came from beyond. "Are you all right?" Michael's voice had risen several notches.

Sounds of heavy breathing. "Yes, yes."

Michael froze. The words were muffled, strained and stressed. The vocal cords themselves might have been pureed. But yes yes? "Dad?" he asked incredulously. He stared at the door like the contestant on a game show waiting to see if he'd be a winner.

He heard a click as the door unlocked from within and the copper handle turned counterclockwise.

The door swung open.

A winner.

"Hi, Son," said Taft, doing his best to manage an air of nonchalant ease. He grinned a wooden grin. "Need to use the bathroom? I'm finished." Taft gritted his upper teeth to his lowers and swallowed flecks of bilious debris.

Michael stuck his head in the bathroom. The stench of death slammed him. He expected to see a mule, half decomposed and breeding fly eggs and beetles. There was nothing. Just the monogrammed guest towels. A fresh bar of soap. And his father.

"What's going on?" asked Michael.

There are over thirty-five million gastric glands in the stomach. The homebrewed gastric juice therein contains a gastric lipase, hydrochloric acid, mucin, pepsin, rennin and water, with a pH of about one. The stomach, a smooth muscle bag, is capable of experiencing an increase in content without an increase in pressure. This is accommodation.

Taft's body was not being very accommodating these days. The Law of Laplace says that the greater the diameter of a tube, the less pressure required to distend it. Taft's body was breaking all the rules these days. And he felt like his pH was about minus twelve.

Michael was staring at him. Did Taft dare a discourse on physics and applied biology? Should he allow himself to faint instead, thereby forestalling if not circumventing the inevitable?

"I'm dying," Taft said. Oops.

Now, kinship is a funny thing. Some societies are patrilineal. Others are matrilineal. Modern Western society is largely bilateral. That is to say, we view our mother's kinfolk to be equally important as our father's kin. In some societies, all of a woman's sisters, female cousins, et cetera, are called sisters. An aunt or distant female collateral may be called mother. Each male of a man's generation may be called brother.

Respect. Respect for kinship is nearly universal. Very few peoples toss out their old or any of their kin for that matter. Even the modern Westerner, for all his callousness, is only cold-blooded enough to banish his parents to a retirement home, yet still sends them birthday and Christmas cards as necessary and for as long as the Social Security checks hold up.

So when Michael had the base urge to punch out his father we must be understanding. Love and kinship, fear and death. They make a strange brew. All the witches in Salem wouldn't have the power to neutralize that concoction.

Michael balled up his fists but never raised his hands.

Taft stood in fear. In fear of his own son. And he was too shocked to move or even dodge to one side. A millisecond later Michael was on him. Hugging him so hard that Taft was certain Michael was trying to kill him, when all he was really doing was trying to keep his father alive. . .

# 30

Ten trillion cells in his body and one damned nucleic acid rung goes bad and screws everything up. Valine instead of glycine, who'd have thought it would have made such a difference? Taft was dying of cancer. That is, his liver was being consumed by the uncontrolled growth of cells. One faulty switch and his life was being taken from him. As Marie's had been taken from her, from him. Now the malignancy had spread to his colon.

President Nixon declared war on cancer. Little did Taft realize that war would take place inside him. And he'd voted for the man. The doctor said that soon Taft would not be able to eat, his insides were so clogged with cancer. Then they would hook him to an IV trickling sugar and vitamins and high doses of morphine. And then it would be only a question of what gave out first. His mind, his heart, his liver, his intestines?

Or would it be the deathly pain he would feel when the morphine had reached a level beyond which it would cease helping him and would kill him itself?

Oh, and just before leaving Florida, when he'd gone to Doctor Johnston's (he couldn't go to Dr. Cobeur for fear that Marie would find out about his own cancer) office for a checkup and to refill the chemo-pump that they'd surgically implanted beside his liver, he'd found out that the crick in his neck was not a cramp or the result a too soft pillow nor even was it caused by his craning his neck to watch the gentle walk of a pretty girl from Ipanema and ports south. The cancer had spread to his bone. Shot up from his liver to his neck like a murderer in the night who kills and kills again.

Only this time, this murderer was killing the same victim

over and over again. Jack the Ripper had nothing on him. Jack was an amateur. Get a job, Jack.

Einstein sighed. Though he was a naturalized American citizen, that sigh was heavily accented. It was a sigh of ennui. Some days the photodimension could be so tedious. Maybe he should start thinking about taking a vacation. . .

"What's going on Dad? What are you talking about?" Michael's troubled face stared back at him from the bathroom mirror.

Taft nearly cried. It had been a long time since Michael had reached out to him. If he'd had to pay for that with his life, he believed it would be equitable. "Cancer, Michael." He held his son at arm's length. "I'm afraid I've got the cancer."

Michael gasped. "I don't believe it, I mean, you can't." Michael refused to believe. If he believed this, he'd likely have to believe all kinds of other bad things. Things that he'd never considered, never let into his life or his mind. Let one in and they all want in. Keep everything out. It was the rule he'd lived by.

"It's the way things go go," said Taft. He'd had lots of time to get used to the idea.

"H-how long?" muttered Michael. Another minute in the cloistered bathroom and he believed he'd vomit.

Taft did mental calculations. "About eight months."

Michael shook his head disbelieving.

Taft dried his hands on the pristine pink towel with the 'Jensens' embroidered inscription. He stepped past his son and stood in the center of the bedroom.

Michael turned and watched him.

Taft spoke. "You remember when I had my appendix out last summer?"

Michael nodded.

"Chemo-pump."

"What?"

"Chemo-pump. It's some kinda dealy they installed beside my liver. The doctor shoots the drugs into it and over a period of a few days it's released into my body. I need refills every few days, sometimes I can go a week." Taft held a hand to his side. "You can feel it here," he said. "It kind of sticks out a bit."

Michael shuddered noticeably. "Your appendix?"

"Still got it," said his father. "That was just the excuse I told everybody, well—"

"Well what?"

"The girls knew. I didn't tell you or Marie. I couldn't tell Marie."

Michael nearly screamed. Then he did scream. "WHY DIDN'T YOU TELL ME?"

Taft recoiled though he'd been expecting the sonic boom. He shrugged. He spoke sotto voce. The words barely leaked out. "I didn't think you'd care. . ."

Michael danced around the bedroom like a springbok. If he'd been a gazelle, he'd have set new records for the high jump. "And now, jumping for the University of California at Santa Barbara, Michael Springbok Hart. He's leaving the blocks. He leaps. Fourteen feet seven and three-eighths inches, a new world's record!"

Gazelles everywhere exchanged dollars as wagers were settled. Joe Gazelle lost his watch (Rolex) to a water buffalo from New Delhi. He'd bet that Michael wouldn't clear thirteen feet. He didn't think Michael's bones were delicate enough. The water buffalo would later sell the watch (Rolex) on the black market.

As it is, Michael paced angrily, nervously, unsteadily. Why did his father always do these things to him? Why couldn't he be a normal father and stop trying to make him and everyone around him crazy? The next thing he remembered was the sound of breaking glass.

Had he thrown the stiff wooden chair through the soon to be yielding glass door? Yep. You betcha. Oh yeah.

Taft ran to his son, who stood shivering against the incoming coldness. The icy, wet wind blew in like a dark opponent with a whetted saber who'd found his opening and attacked swiftly with determination and vengeance.

# 31

Darkness consumed the house except for one light, a brass table lamp beside a ridiculously large and horribly overstuffed sofa. Michael sat at the end of the fattened sofa closest to the one-hundred-watt light, hands on knees. He wasn't feeling so good.

Cora and Troy, Michael's father, Elizabeth and Martin, and Mary stood hovering nearby, like a tribe of hill people. Like the Ona from Tierra del Fuego gathered round the campfire to consider the ethnologist who'd fallen inescapably into their collective lap.

Christie and Judy were in Cora and Troy's bedroom watching big-screen TV.

Michael wasn't catatonic, merely vegetative. He'd have given anything at all to be home in California just then.

"Should we leave him here?" asked Martin. He'd never had a brother-in-law go nuts on him before. What did the etiquette books say?

Cora shrugged. "There's plenty of space, except that he's burst a hole in the guest room."

"Michael," said Mary, "Would you like to come stay with me for a few days?"

Michael managed a look, though what it meant was unclear to everyone. His sister, Mary, was speaking to him. She looked more like Michael than anyone else in the family. They could have been twins. He understood her. Like him, she lived alone and had never married. She was a school teacher, taught high school history.

"No." He nearly collapsed. It was the first word he'd managed in an hour. Everybody had gone home except for immediate family.

Mary looked helplessly at her father. Taft cleared his throat. "Well—" he said.

"Can I borrow a car?"

"What?" Cora and Elizabeth asked simultaneously.

"I'd like to borrow somebody's car," repeated Michael looking from one to the next of kin. They looked like bowling pins from where he sat. Six pins standing. He could take them out with one toss of that big, grotesque sculpture over there by the fireplace, he surmised. Maybe two shots at best. He'd have to be careful though or he'd end up with a seven-ten split. That could get tricky.

"Sure, take mine," offered Martin. He pulled a small leather case with the General Motors logo on its front out of his pants pocket and handed it to Michael.

Michael gripped the keycase in his pale fingers. "Thanks." He rose recklessly and bumped the table with his shins. The brass lamp wobbled as if to say 'Watch it, buddy.'

Outside the front door, he stopped and adjusted his collar. His tie hung half-open about his neck and the top button had come unfastened. His white shirt fell in loose folds over his pants. It was so cold he thought it might snow. Martin's car was down the drive and along the street behind Mary's.

Michael jogged down the hill and experimented with three keys before happening upon the right one. He jumped behind the wheel and closed the door. The car was a cold coffin of steel. He drove through the rain which fell like superstrings, passing alien universes left and right. Even if he'd had a map it would have done him no good. He got lost three times and it had taken him nearly three hours to find it. There were no lights shining in any windows. There were no reading lamps in use by late night page turners. No glow from even a single electron soup machine sloshing out entertainment. The cemetery sat dark.

He left Martin's car beside the curb on the main street. It would be safe there. There were hardly any cars coming this way this night. The drizzle pummeled like fine needles puncturing his skin. Tacks on a drum.

The iron gate he climbed was frigid under his fingers. He worked his way past all the dead souls whom he'd never known until he found his mother's grave. She was there. She was still there. The headstone was proof of that.

The ground was still filled in. Fresh, cultivated green sod had been laid overtop as if to hide the fact that Marie was only freshly entombed. But it didn't match up to the dead brown grass surrounding it. The only thing missing was the flowers. There had been so many flowers there that afternoon that they'd spilled out from the tent and into the rain.

Someone had taken the flowers.

# 32

Alex went past Taft's empty house and peered at the garden. Somebody had to water all those flowers. The lawn, too, was looking brown. There wasn't much rain even in Florida this time of year. Lake Okeechobee itself wished she could slake her growing, unabating thirst. The crows complained loudly and the bass bemoaned the loss of valuable square footage.

Alex glanced at his plastic watch. He still had time before school. He put on the brakes and parked his Schwinn beside the house. The garden hose was wrapped up like a cobra in the gravel beneath the side window.

Alex turned on the spigot and pulled the heavy green hose along beside him. With the expert thumb work that comes from experience, he directed a cold blast of water at Marie's garden. The flowers seemed to raise their heads and say "What's up, Alex?"

The boy gave the back lawn a scattered blast for good measure and returned the hose to the house, coiling it as neatly as he could manage. He washed his soiled hands and took a swallow of water before turning off the faucet. On the way home from school he would stop by again and collect the newspaper and the mail. Sometimes there were handbills stuck in the door. He took those, too.

Looking himself over he noticed that his red canvas sneakers were damp and dirty. His pants were damp too, but they would dry by the time he reached school. He jumped on his bike and barreled off.

Somewhere in the house Einstein paced restlessly. He hated it when everybody went out and left him home alone.

# 33

Elizabeth gently knuckled the bedroom door. "Telephone, Michael."

"Who is it?" came the glum reply.

"I don't know. A woman." Elizabeth knew exactly who was on the line. How could she not know? She'd dialed the number herself.

Michael came out of his room looking more crumpled than the bed sheets and picked up the portable receiver. "Hello," he said emotionlessly.

"Hello, Michael. It's me, Ellen. From Brooksville, you know —"

"Oh, sure," said Michael. What on earth did she want? He idly traced his ear with his index finger while waiting to hear what she wanted of him. Michael did not believe in people calling just to say hello.

"I just wanted to say hello."

Michael frowned.

"And I wanted to let you know that Alex has been taking very good care of your father's house while he's away. How is your father by the way?" Oops, Elizabeth had told her about Michael's finding out about the illness and Ellen had promised not to mention that she also had known about Taft's seemingly hopeless condition. But then, life itself was a fatal condition.

"Fine," said Michael. He had no idea what Ellen knew or did not know and he didn't care.

"Will you be staying in Brooksville long after you get back?"

"I really don't know," replied Michael. Long uncomfortable pause. "I should get back to work."

"Yes, of course. I—well, if you were going to be around for a few days I thought I could show you the beach?" There, she'd said it and now she was sure that even her toenails were blushing with embarrassment. Perhaps even her spleen. Could spleens blush?

Michael didn't know what to say. "That's not necessary."

Ellen could have choked him. "I know it's not necessary," she replied, fighting to steady her voice and her temper. What she really felt like doing was screaming. Screaming loud enough that Michael would end up with a black and blue ear from the sheer force of her cry.

Elizabeth hovered nearby and Michael turned his back to her. Elizabeth stuck out her tongue at him.

"If you change your mind—"

"I just don't see the point."

"The point is to have some fun. Both you and your father could use some." She didn't mean to admonish him. But she had. Oh well. Served him right. And maybe it would do him some good.

"Yes." Michael stumbled over the social graces. "You're right," he said, thinking of his father.

In the end, he promised to telephone or drop by the minute he and his father returned to Florida. Ellen came away happy and Elizabeth, who phoned Ellen back only minutes later to confabulate, came away quite satisfied as well.

# 34

Taft decided to enter the stream.

Now some people enter the stream straight on, with no regard for currents or the depth of the water. They don't even touch the water to test whether it is cool or tepid. They don't study the direction of the flow or consider whether or not they can see bottom. They just plunge straight ahead.

In you go!

Sometimes they take off their shoes and socks and roll up their pant legs. But that's the best they can do. All else is left to chance or destiny depending upon your view of things.

Some people enter at an oblique or look for the narrowest spot to cross and they want to know which way the water is flowing, so they toss a stick in first to see which way it travels and how fast. If they can find a big enough stick, they test the depth of the water as far out as they can reach and they become doubly cautious if the water is muddy and they can't see what's lurking beneath the surface.

There could be rocks, sharp and cold; wet, corpulent weeds that could ensnare and trap unsuspecting water crossers, maybe even unscrupulous denizens such as crocodiles with long triangular snouts and sixty interlocking meat-rending teeth, and piranha or hollow-fanged water moccasins just waiting for you to take your chances. They would then take theirs.

Some people enter streams as a matter of course. Life seems to be going along in one direction or another and suddenly they find themselves entering one stream or another and off they go!

It's not sure whether they ever had any choice in the matter or if they would even choose to have a choice in the decision. In fact, such entering of streams seems to be more a question of convergence rather than conscious decision or action taking.

Somehow a certain stream just happened to be in their path as a result of about a bazillion other occurrences, chances and decisions. So off they went, rolling up their pant legs and pausing (but for only a second) to test the water. They plunged ahead. Because they knew that was the way life went. Ahead.

If the man on the street had asked Taft (who happened himself to be walking up the street from his house to Ellen and Alex's house) if he were about to enter a stream, Taft would definitely have answered no. He was not about to enter a stream. At least (taking a quick look around) not that he was aware of.

He and Michael had been home for nearly a week and still the Michigan chill had not left his bones. He had adjusted to many things in life. Work, children, marriage, death. And so many more. Taft went to Ellen and Alex's house nearly every afternoon now. It was a new habit. A new routine that kept him going. Besides, he was pilfering her medicine cabinet.

As he left her house afterward, Ellen reminded Taft of the impending picnic expedition to the coast that was set for Saturday morning.

"Wouldn't miss it, miss it," promised Taft.

"Good," replied Ellen. "It'll do both of you good. You need to get out. Keep busy. Believe me," she said quite believably, "I know."

Taft nodded. "I'll remind Michael."

Ellen glanced down the street in the direction of Taft's house. "What's he been doing? I don't see him around much since the two of you got back. Last time I saw him outdoors was two or three days ago when he cut the lawn."

Taft shrugged. "Don't remind me. He had adjusted the mower blades so low that he cut through roots and all. The entire lawn is in shock shock and will most likely have to be replanted."

Ellen laughed. It felt good to laugh, so Taft joined her.

"Michael means well. He helps me out, you know. And he's got his work. Doing research, he says." Taft stuck his hands in his pockets. "Well, I'll see you in the morning."

"Right. We'll come by around eight or eight-thirty. Alex is so excited. He asks me about it every day. Sometimes that boy makes me crazy."

Taft smiled.

# 35

Taft knocked on Michael's door. "Son?" he called experimentally.

"Yeah, Dad, come on in."

Michael sat at his desk staring over notes and black-and-white photographs taken at an archaeological dig.

"Didn't mean to interrupt your work," apologized Taft.

"No problem." Michael pushed the papers away from his sight and straightened up in the stiff pine, Shaker-style chair. "Do you need anything?"

Taft shook his head no. He fondled the glass paperweight that Marie had allowed their daughter Mary to purchase in Gatlinburg, Tennessee, back when they were in the Great Smoky Mountains one summer on two weeks' vacation. It had been sitting on that desk, Mary's old school desk, for years.

When Taft and Marie moved down to Florida, they'd reassembled that desk, paperweight and all. Except for some tiny scratches the paperweight had held up remarkably well. A 1907 Buffalo head nickel was embedded in the center of the weight. The coin remained in perfect condition. Chief Two Guns Whitecalf had never looked better. If you broke the paperweight that nickel would probably be worth some real money.

"Whatcha working on, son?"

"Same thing. My report on the dig from last summer." He'd spent part of the past summer living off canned goods while digging up the hills around San Luis Potosi and months later was still trying to make sense of the data.

"It must be hard trying to keep up on your work from here," said Taft. It was a tentative statement. He tried to sneak it in between the ribs. Like a quick, bloodless thrust.

Michael flared back. "Dad, I don't even want to hear about it. Don't start going on about that again. I've made up my mind." He stopped and caught his breath. "I'm sorry, Dad." He was genuinely sorry. "I didn't mean to snap at you."

After all, he'd decided to stay in Florida and take a leave of absence from his job because of his desire to help his father. "But we've been all through this. I can take a leave of absence. It's no big problem. Besides, I made the decision to do this. I want to. End of story."

Taft bit his lip. "I just don't want to be in the way."

"You're not in the way."

"I could move into the hospice."

"They'd probably throw you out the first time they heard you practicing on that ancient concertina of yours." Michael grinned. "Don't you see? This is the way things were meant to be."

"Yes, yes," agreed Taft. "The way things are meant to be."

Now supposing you'd shot and roasted a nice juicy, fat-soaked mammoth for dinner (mammuthus imperator). You and your buddies have ingested all but the toenails. Ummm, that bone marrow was delicious, wasn't it? You're in something of a stupor. An after-dinner walk seems to be in order. Off you go skipping merrily over rock and fen. Haplessly, you've gone too far, skipped right past the pre-projectile point horizon and ended up on the cusp of the Laurentide Glacier. No way you can tell the missus you stayed out late fishing with the boys, boasting about the iron-toothed fish that got away. After all, Lake Michigan is but a dream in God's eye. All of the so-called Great Lakes are nothing more than glacial exudate. Yuck. Who'd want to go fishing in that?

Poor Saquarema Gomes (S.G. to his friends) of the Howell Gomes' of Long Island, New York, he's gone and screwed up good now. Still, he got a good meal out of the deal. And for all the lack of civilization and its perks, he didn't have to worry about Miss Manners or washing the dishes. He rubbed his dirty hide in the dirt (more for fun than cleanliness) and he tossed his old bones in the midden (no dishwashers, no soap, no bother). S.G. had the good life. No doubt.

Ernie Hart had the good life, too. Okay, so his real God-given name was Ernest. Nobody ever called him that, including his mother, because everyone knew that the last thing in the world that Ernie was was E/earnest. That's with a capital E or a little e. Ernie was neither. Ernie grew up to be a fisherman. It's a good thing because he spent all day on a boat with a net sifting lake water and lines dangling bait. If he'd been a vacuum cleaner salesman, he'd be having a hell of a time paying his mortgage and electric bill. Ernie fished the Great Lakes. This was a time when the Great Lakes were just that, Great. Ernie loved those lakes. Ernie didn't collect dust, he collected trout. If you wanted to see Ernie you had to go see those lakes because that was where you'd always find Ernie.

Taft, Ernie's older brother by two and two-tenths years, visited him often. Ernie and Taft were close. Ernie never finished high school. How could he when there were so many trout to catch?

Now the powers-that-be built the Welland Ship Canal linking Lake Ontario and Lake Erie. Of course, neither the Canadians nor the Americans consulted the trout on this matter. Hell, they didn't even ask Ernie and he spent all day, six days of the week on those lakes.

The lamprey eel of the Agnathan class is a primitive sort. Oh, they have two-chambered hearts, senses of sight and smell and the finest notochord you've ever seen, but all in all they're simple folk. For years the lamprey eels had bemoaned the lack of an open channel to the Great Lakes from the sea. Petitions went round. Polls were taken. But nothing got done until the Americans and the Canadians decided to take matters into their own opposable-thumbed hands. And what better hands to do it? Even the lampreys had to concede this point. After all, the lampreys barely maintained equilibrium let alone balanced a shovel in one hand while smoking a hand-rolled cigarette in the other, while taking an unauthorized coffee break.

The oral sucker department. That's where their strength lies. Roll over, Linda Lovelace. Their mouths contain piston-like tongues with tooth-like projections which can rasp holes in the skin of any host. The tongue creates suction when the cartilage rimmed mouth is placed against an object (like your hide) and drawn back. They even build nests for egg laying by carrying and piling up rocks that they haul with their mouths. The lamprey respires through a set of seven openings on each side of its snakish, yard-long body.

Now, the first thing that all those lampreys did when the route to the Great Lakes was finally inaugurated was to exclaim "Wow, look at all those trout!" Soon the two (lampreys and trout) became quite attached to one another. Body fluid and blood flowed from trout to lamprey. Trout got very little out of this deal. (I mean, more pain they didn't need.) Lampreys change hosts often. They injured their hosts more often than they killed them. Which is exactly what most of one's houseguests do to their hosts.

Regardless, in 1939, Ernie Hart and his friends pulled over a million pounds of trout from Lake Huron. Just how many tons were Ernie's has never been sorted out. By 1951, only a few pounds of trout were reportedly fished out of the lake. But by this time, Ernie had moved on up the road to Lake Michigan where, in 1945, he and his new friends plucked better than five million tons of gamy trout from that lake. Unfortunately, only four hundred pounds or so were caught in that same lake less than ten years later.

Ernie and his friends were out of work. Ernie found a job working on a laker (long narrow ships built specifically for hauling freight across the lakes) carrying grain which came from the upper Midwest and was being sent on to Buffalo, New York, for processing. Some of that grain was processed into alcohol which Ernie drank earnestly. Until he died of acute alcoholic poisoning, that is. They buried his body in the podzolic soil of Cheboygan (just about on the tip of the middle finger of the left hand of that mitten called Michigan) because Ernie had always said that he should be buried dead wherever he last stood alive. That was Cheboygan. Lucky Cheboygan.

Ernie was pretty wise. Ernie made a lot of sense for being only thirty-six years old when he more or less killed himself. Taft entered one stream. Lampreys entered another and young Ernie entered a third. Maybe it was all just one stream after all but things just got so mixed up you couldn't tell.

Now this whole ugly incident could (conceivably) have been avoided had Ernie and his friends convinced the world that what they really wanted was eels. After all, the lowly eel had been considered a delicacy in the Middle Ages. Why not now? Now being circa 1950. Apparently, all this was, to quote both Taft and his son for double effect, "The way things were meant to be."

"I wouldn't mind," said Taft, "being in some hospice."

"Forget it," said Michael.

A long silence hung over the room, as if waiting for a curtain call that would not come.

"Ellen said to remind you about tomorrow—"

"Right, I haven't forgotten," Michael knew how much it meant to his dad. Taft loved the Gulf. His father may not have had the sea in his blood as thick as Uncle Ernie had, but it was there nevertheless. Perhaps it was in everyone, a vestige of our days as lower forms on the evolutionary ladder as we scuttled through the mud testing the nitrogen rich air.

# 36

Michael ate his dinner, quietly, standing in the kitchen, while his father sat in the living room reading The Three Musketeers by Dumas. One of those books he'd always meant to read. When you know you are dying, there is so much to get done. The room was dark except for the light over his chair. Taft could barely manage to eat any longer. Nothing went through. Whatever went down he had to vomit back up. At best he could manage bits of ice that he let slowly dissolve in his mouth. The rest of the time he had to hook up the IV, which at the moment hung on its steel frame beside his easy chair.

Maybe, Taft thought, looking at that chair at the odd moment, hooked to his life dripping plastic tubes, he should change the name of that chair. Life wasn't so easy now. Maybe he'd change its name to the hard chair. The I'm-getting-sicker-by-the-minute chair and soon-I'm-going-to-die chair. The how-much-pain-can-you-stand-before-you-go chair. . .

# 37

Ellen was nervous. Alex was charged up, like a race car waiting for the flag to wave, the race to begin. She'd finally settled on pink culottes and a pair of new leather sandals after much taking on and putting off and mirror judging and hair fixing.

Alex had simply put on the same clothes he'd worn the afternoon before. They'd been hanging on the back of his door and they still looked good to him.

Alex helped his mom carry the picnic cooler and water jug. They took some folding chairs and a beach umbrella and a big old blanket stored in the garage.

Michael had put on a pair of khaki trouser and a white knit pullover. He was tying his shoes when he heard the blare of the car horn. "I got it!" He stood. "You ready, Dad?" he called from his room.

His father shouted some words that were too muffled to understand. Michael peeked out the curtains and saw Ellen and Alex together in the front seat. Ellen spotted him and waved. Michael did a half-wave back. "It's them."

Taft came around from the hall. He had on his trousers and his shirt was hanging out by the tails. He wore socks and slippers.

"Dad," exclaimed Michael, "how come you're not ready? They're here."

"Sorry, Michael," said Taft, heavily. "Not feeling too too well." He gave Michael a gamey look. "Guess I'll have to pass for today."

"But—" Michael was about to tell his father that he had to come, then realized how horrible it would sound. Pushing around a dying man and one's father to boot was not exactly the advice of Miss Manners. "I'll tell her you're not feeling well."

Michael put his hand on the doorknob. "She'll understand." Taft nodded. "I'll tell her we'll have to make it another time." Michael turned to go.

"No!" said Taft. He shifted from foot to foot like a bull waiting to charge. "I mean, you can still go."

"I can't leave you home alone, you know that. Especially if you're feeling worse today."

"It's just my stomach," argued his father, as if there were only a 'just' to it. "I don't feel up to a road trip, that's all. I'll be okay if I stay around the house. No need to worry about me. You'd be letting Ellen and Alex down if you didn't go," Taft said. Rub a little guilt in for good measure.

"She's gone to a lot of trouble. Or disappoint the boy. Besides," Taft said, "It's Saturday, there're plenty of people around that I can call if I get into trouble."

Taft opened the front door and barged outside. "Come on," he said. "It'll do you good to get out of the house. Good morning, Ellen," he called from the stoop.

Ellen said hello. Michael and his father walked down to the car. Michael wasn't feeling so well himself suddenly. What was he going to say to Ellen and Alex for a whole day? He had little enough to speak about with his own father.

"Hi," Michael said nervously.

"Ready?" asked Ellen, noticing Taft in his slippers.

"Afraid not," answered Taft. "Stomach's bothering me. I'll have to pass. But not to worry worry, Michael's still going, dying to."

Michael managed to fake a smile.

"Are you sure?" said Ellen.

"Sure sure," Taft replied. "You go on ahead. I'll sit and read. Maybe beat on the old concertina without anybody around to complain about me making their skin crawl," he joked.

"Well . . ."

Alex opened the passenger side door and hopped out. "I'll

stay here with Mister Hart."

"Alex, I don't know—" started Ellen.

"Why thanks, Alex, son," interposed Taft quickly. A little too quickly for Michael's peace of mind. "That'd be swell. I could use some company. And then," he said to his son, "you really wouldn't have to worry about me. Alex will take take care of me. Won't you, Alex?"

"Yeah," answered Alex. He'd already removed his backpack from the rear seat and was leading Michael by one paralyzed forearm to the car. Michael sat down beside Ellen but refrained from looking at her.

Ellen smiled anxiously. "I guess we'll be off."

"Have fun!" called Taft with a wave.

"Bye, Mom! Bye, Michael!"

The car seemed to disappear around the corner. Though this was only an illusion. Somewhere around the corner, that car bearing Michael and Ellen continued on and to the passengers the illusion was that the man and child on the sidewalk had disappeared.

"Well," said Taft proudly, "that went rather well."

"Yep," answered Alex, picking his backpack up from the driveway. "Just like you said it would." He ran up the lawn. "We still going to the carnival?"

A traveling carnival had come to town and set up over on the vacant lot next to the Baptist church. It was in town for three days. Friday, Saturday and Sunday.

"You betcha."

# 38

Ellen drove with great method.

Ploddingly.

Almost afraid to hurry up or to slow down. The trip to the beach was only fifteen miles long. Even so, Michael had a hard time sticking to the seat. Ellen's car was one of those big old Chevy Novas, not one of those compact new ones. And the seats were shiny and slick. Not even the seatbelt knotted about his waist seemed to hold him in one spot and he was deathly afraid of sliding into Ellen across the way. Michael feared physical contact.

Old car seats either caved in and became too soft or they got hard and slick like those in Ellen's car. There seemed to be no in-between. Didn't anything age gracefully anymore?

A slow-moving, green tractor up ahead, more at home in a field of mud than on a paved highway, had created a line of stalled cars in the opposite lane. One after the other, they passed the hapless tractor as it bounced along the side of the highway. The tractor's driver was as skinny as a bird-pecked scarecrow and had the tiniest human head Michael had ever seen. The tractor driver's head was so small that from a distance he looked like the Headless Horseman himself. The Headless Horseman with an avocado between his shoulders.

Two cars decided to go at once and the distance between the second car and Ellen's car closed quickly. Ellen inadvertently drove onto the shoulder, perhaps subconsciously trying to create more space between herself and the car in the oncoming lane. The shoulder was rough. Michael bounced like a bronco rider at the Denver Rodeo International Event.

Ellen's black ceramic travel coffee mug perched on the

dashboard. It was a gift from the bank where she kept her checking account. The mug was one of those with the squat bottom and the slender orifice. Not unlike many cultish female figurines which Michael had dug up in his researches.

The cup slid down the dashboard along the window then bounced upward as Ellen's front tires encountered a pothole. Ceramic bounced off windshield glass and the coffee cup became a flying missile. Coffee spewed out like the last coughs of Mt. Saint Helen's. Chocolate-colored lava rained up, hit the roof and then rained down. Drops clung to the roof of the car and fell arrhythmically on their heads. The cup rebounded off the front bench seat and rolled lifelessly on its side as Ellen restored the car to the pavement.

"God, I'm sorry," she said rather abashedly.

"That's all right," Michael managed to reply. He leaned forward, one hand on the dash lest Ellen take to the shoulder once again, bashing his head against the dashboard instruments and perhaps lodging him up to his neck in the glove box. He picked up the travel mug, which had certainly become more traveled now, and righted it. He left it on the floorboard. It was empty after all. His shoes were damp and his white socks were spotted brown.

By comparison, the sand fleas, fire ants and rain they encountered at the coast were a blessing. The waters of the Gulf were as smooth as the glass of the Hubble space telescope, which is to say smooth, but not that smooth. Michael watched his reflection change shape in the water. He studied the action of the fluid. The tide didn't seem to know whether it was coming in or going out.

In 1957, a pleasure craft had gone down in the Gulf about midway between Pascagoula and St. Petersburg. On board were a young professor of physics and his bride. They'd been caught in a squall and the boat had tipped fiercely to one side letting in an inescapable amount of saltwater. The storm was so loud that they never even heard each other screaming. Einstein had heard every word. But what could he do, stuck as he was?

The young professor possessed an autographed photograph taken of Einstein one winter in Massachusetts. Einstein had been one of his mentors. The young professor was as proud of that photograph as he was of his new boat. The boat even came with a guarantee. A little late for that now. Einstein was conjoined to the murky depths. His photograph was safe behind the sturdy, watertight glass frame. Once he'd spotted an interesting small specimen of a variety of fish that he'd never seen before.

How he wished for a Dell Pocket Guide of Fishes at times like these. This particular fish was red with blue lips and had several tiny fins along each side of its flattish body. The tiny, red fish had been tagging along behind a school of some big brown things. Another fish he did not know. Albert had only viewed this lone red fish the one time and he might never see it again.

Michael tested the water with his toes. Very warm. He looked up and down the beach and was surprised that it was as unoccupied as it was. In California, people cluttered the beaches, so much so that you could smell the choking scent of suntan oil over the smell of the sea itself. Ellen was setting a cloth over a picnic table across the sand among a tiny stand of pines and scrub.

Only one other couple was visible in the park. An older couple with a Winnebago. One of those big types, at least thirty foot. Both the man and the woman had gray hair. Their poodle had white hair. Hard to say who was older.

They had set up one of those folding aluminum tables outside the door of the Winnebago. The woman kept entering and exiting the camper bearing food from the oven. The man threw scraps off each plate to the dog.

"Good morning," said the white-haired man to Michael as he passed by.

"Hello," said Michael.

"Nice day for the beach." The man tossed out the words like he tossed bones to his poodle.

Michael barely broke stride. "Yes," he said, the man now

safely behind him. "It is." Cripes, why couldn't people keep to themselves? he wondered.

"Not going in?" Ellen had laid everything out on the table while Michael was taking his walk along the break-line.

"In a bit." He sat down on the stained and weathered picnic bench across from Ellen. Across the potato chips, cole slaw, apple crisps and ham salad. A fresh loaf of sourdough bread, a bottle of inexpensive white wine from a vintner in the Santa Ynez region of California (not far from Michael's current home of Santa Barbara) and a perspiring jug of fresh-squeezed orange juice completed the scene.

Michael poured himself a glass of orange juice.

Ellen had removed her shirt. Her bikini top was rose red and her skin was lightly tanned. Ellen's breasts seemed to hang weightlessly, unblemished and large as softballs. He could see the outline of her nipples through the skimpy fabric.

Ellen followed Michael's gaze and blushed. She looked into his face and Michael realized with dismay that she'd caught him staring at her breasts. He blushed as well. Except that his was the only blush to show. Deeply and utterly. Ellen's skin held just enough brown and the flush didn't reveal itself. Michael was pale by contrast and his embarrassment painted itself across his face like watercolors spelling out the fact that this was a lecherous fool.

He felt like an idiot.

Ellen laughed self-consciously to break the uneasy tension and fiddled with a plastic fork. Michael grabbed the potato chip bag and broke it open.

"Shall we eat?"

"Okay," said Michael, reaching into the oily, foil package. "Everything looks great. The food, I mean."

Ellen giggled. "I know what you meant."

Afterward, they drank coffee from Ellen's Thermos, the same one she'd loaned Michael and his father when they'd gone to Michigan, and took a walk up the beach. The poodle followed them to the water before its owner could coax it back to the land of the Winnebago.

Ellen had taken off her shorts by this time and Michael was surprised at how good she looked. The muscles of her buttocks and legs flexed and tautened like those of a dancer with each step she took.

Michael stripped down to his UCSB gym shorts. Both were barefoot. The sand was hot, but not so bad if they stuck to the tide line. They walked past the sea and the clouds and the terns. Several times they'd spotted dolphin jumping in the space between the horizon and the shore.

Ellen took his hand in the middle of that oceanic silence. Michael responded by swallowing so hard that he (for a second) believed he'd swallowed his tongue. He followed up this remarkable feat by another. He tripped.

On the smooth, obstacle-less, unhazarded by mine fields or camouflaged beach chairs, vast expanse of Florida beach, Michael tripped.

Face deep in the sand, saltwater splashing in his eyes and leaking in his ears, he faced the inevitable consequence of having to get up again. Oh great. Just great. For the second time in the afternoon, he had to look like an idiot.

"Michael," said Ellen leaning downward. "Are you all right?"

Michael groaned noncommittally.

"Let me help you up."

Michael twisted his head, now flecked with trillions of bits of sand and seashell, toward Ellen. There were those breasts again, nearly in his face. He felt his body grow against the sand. His loins obscenely nudging Mother Nature.

"I'll manage," he croaked, suppressing the urge to nuzzle his face against her chest. Something about the hot sun and the sea brought out this animal urge in him. Perhaps it was a primordial memory from days long ago when some ancestral relation of man's was crawling out of the sea to fornicate on the beach and do its part for evolution.

Ellen grabbed his arm and lifted while Michael pushed off

with his free arm.

"You okay?"

"Yeah, I'm fine." Except that he now looked like a giant, appendaged piece of sandpaper with a muck-filled mouth and two salt-ravaged eyeballs.

Ellen reached over and wiped wet sand from his lips. "You'd better rinse off."

"This would be a good time for that swim," agreed Michael, trying to flesh bits of sand out of his teeth with his tongue even as he was speaking.

Ellen and Michael waded out into the warm waters of the Gulf. The water was now up to Michael's knees. Michael dove. He wanted to shake off his embarrassment and agitation as much as he wanted to shake off the imagined feel of Ellen's breasts and the all too real prickling sand that was itching his skin in places seen and unseen.

He dove again. With a kick and a leap, up and out, into the water hard, at a seventy-degree angle.

And, what the hell is this sandbar doing here? he thought, just before he passed out upon slamming into that well-hidden sand barrier with his hands and face.

With great ignominy would he forever remember the day when Ellen pulled him limping and stupid with concussion and humiliation from the sea. If saltwater were hemlock, he'd be dead as Socrates.

# 39

"You all right?"

"Yes," said Michael, more embarrassed than sore. "It's only a sprained neck."

"You're lucky," said Taft. "You might have drowned." He scooped up the plastic control that worked the hospital bed. "You want me to adjust this thing?"

"No," the reply came quickly. Michael strained to sit up. The pillows were way too soft. He wanted to go home.

"He gets to stay overnight," said Alex. "I asked the doctor. He has to go home tomorrow though." He said this with a note of sadness, as if the adventure would be over before it began.

"Yep yep, you're lucky Ellen was there," said Taft.

"It wasn't anything really." Ellen stood beside the bed every bit as embarrassed as Michael. Maybe she shouldn't have brought him to the hospital. Perhaps she should have driven him back to Taft's house as he'd wished. Being rescued by a woman was hardly every man's fantasy. Not that he couldn't have managed to get out on his own. Probably.

"Lucky lucky," Taft said. He plucked a reluctant daisy from the glass vase on the bedside table. A pint-sized pastel blue water pitcher and matching cup, still wrapped in plastic, lay within reach. "Want some?"

Michael shook his head sullenly. He wanted to go home. He needed to go home. He had to take care of his father, not be lying in some stupid hospital bed fretting over a sprained neck and a wounded pride.

Alex played with the remote-control television.

A head popped into the picture. "How we doing?" inquired the sprightly, clear-complexioned, candy stripper, making her usual saccharine rounds.

Michael failed to reply.

"Good, thanks," Ellen responded.

"Okay!"

Like a burst of sugar, she was gone. Off to molest some other bedridden innocent with her cheerful sentiment, thought Michael. It gave him a toothache.

"Maybe we'd better be going," suggested Ellen, the diplomat.

"But it's still early." complained Alex. "Visiting hours aren't over until eight."

"Doesn't matter. I think we'd better let Michael get some rest. We'll come back tomorrow to pick you up. Come on, Alex."

Alex sighed in surrender, turned off the television and returned the control to Michael.

"Thanks," said Michael. "See you tomorrow."

"Goodnight, son," said Taft. "Don't worry about a thing." He reached out a hand to touch Michael's head but withdrew it quickly. It might aggravate Michael's neck pain. Take no chances.

Taft followed Alex out the open door. The corridor was bright and alive with traffic, some walking, some wounded.

"You going to be okay?" Ellen inquired softly. She pulled a chair up next to the edge of the bed and sat.

"Yes, sure," Michael answered. "It's silly really that they want me to stay overnight."

Ellen reached across the blankets and took Michael's left hand. "I'm sorry about this."

"It wasn't your fault."

Ellen shrugged. "Somehow I feel responsible." Ellen twisted her free hand through her scalp. Her hair was stiff from evaporated saltwater.

Ellen had brought Michael directly to the hospital and only went home briefly to pick up Taft and Alex, then returned straight away. Michael had protested the entire drive to the hospital. He wanted only to go home, take a hot shower, swallow a pile of aspirins and get into bed.

But Ellen was fearful that he might have a concussion or some other serious internal injury and had stubbornly brought him to the hospital against his wishes. Ellen was a worrier. Better safe than sorry was a motto she could live with. She'd lost her husband to another's carelessness. She wasn't taking any chances. Not with Michael, not with anyone.

Her hair wouldn't cooperate. Sand and salt stuck to her scalp like a bad shampoo. She knew she was a mess. Her hair was as tangled and poised as an abatis. White sand clung to her legs like minuscule scales and her eyes were red from crying. She hoped Michael didn't notice or, at least, didn't mind.

"Get some rest," she said. "I'll be back in the morning. The doctor on duty said he'd release you tomorrow for sure, so it won't be so bad." She hesitated. "You're not mad at me for bringing you here, are you?"

"No. Of course not."

Ellen stood and the chair was pushed back by the extension of her legs. She bent forward and gave Michael a tentative kiss on the lips. Michael's lips responded, but barely. Yet it was enough for Ellen to take it as encouragement. "Bye," she said, leaving Michael feeling as dizzy as ever.

Michael slept fitfully, as the saying goes. He dreamed of erotic Moche stirrup-spout vessels with spouts molded into the shapes of penises and vulvas, giving the user a choice between fellatio and cunnilingus as the mood took him or her. He dreamed of Ellen wading through the jungles of Tikal wearing only her red bikini digging up Marie's bones beneath a sacred burial altar.

And when she was dug up, she began playing cribbage with Nathaniel Hart who kept trying to distract her (quite ungentlemanly, but good-naturedly) by pumping vigorously away on his accordion. He played polkas, with style. The music carried across the Yucatan and swept like a toy boat bobbing across the wave tops of the Gulf of Mexico until even Albert Einstein caught the subtlest waft of them from his saltwater grave in the cabin cruiser, optimistically christened the Expanding Universe.

Patricia and her father Patrick were diving from their own cabin cruiser, Daddy's Girl. Patrick dove first and Patricia, twenty-years old, and in vigorous good health, followed. Wetsuit bound and scuba gear weighted, she sunk to the bottom, purposefully. There, in tenebrous waters lit only by her diver's lamp, she found the Expanding Universe. The cabin door hung open. What, wondered Einstein, was that light? Some sort of electrified fish?

Patricia, legs kicking as languidly in the water as they would in bed, swam into the interior. Einstein sat up and straightened his tie. He hadn't seen legs like those since Marilyn Monroe. Patricia's light stole across the tiny living quarters and finally landed on Albert. He smiled. Though of course she didn't notice. She did notice the framed picture though and she removed it from its water-rotted perch on the wall. She tucked it into the green mesh bag she carried attached to her diving belt and hurried to the surface to show off her unusual catch to her father.

"Neat, huh?" she exclaimed.

Patrick held the picture up in the air, blocking out the sun. "It's something all right. Looks like a genuine autograph, too." He rubbed the glass with his elbow. "Amazing that the water didn't get into it." He ran a calloused thumb along the edge. It would need reframing.

Albert squinted. It was bright as hell up here after being submerged all these years. Besides, he was terribly upset (as pretty as Patricia was) to leave his Gulf lair. It was the only pair of eyes that he had in the entire region.

"Whatcha gonna do with it?" asked Patrick of his daughter. "Try to sell it?"

"No, I think I'll take it to work with me," said Patricia. Patricia worked as a mermaid. She performed six shows a day at Weeki Wachee, an attraction famous for its underwater mermaid shows.

Einstein had gone and gotten himself rescued by a

mermaid. Who'd have figured?

Patricia made up her mind to hang Einstein's picture in the big aquarium where she swam. She would stick it in the back corner behind the coral where no one but the mermaids could see him. Einstein decided this was a fate he could live with. Beautiful girls cavorting for his secret amusement.

The photodimension could be grueling at times.

# 40

Rebecca fiddled with her pencils and pens. It was going to be one of those long, dull afternoons.

All the professors were out today. Some sort of meeting. And there were no classes. She'd had a letter arrive at the University from her cousin, Michelle, in Maine. It was printed on recycled paper and stuffed into a recycled envelope.

As customary, there was one flat-sided toothpick enclosed with her words. Michelle worked for the Forster Company, manufacturer of white birch toothpicks. They managed to crank out over 600 tons of them each year there by the Sandy River. About 20 billion toothpicks to stick in teeth and maws worldwide. So what if Michelle pilfered one or two and mailed them off in envelopes? Would there be lie detector tests? Internal investigations? Reviews? Toothpick under the fingernail torture?

Rebecca fingered the smooth bit of wood. She hadn't been to Maine in years. Perhaps she could go at Christmas. Michelle would be glad to have her. The last time she'd gone they'd spent time in quaint places like Mooselookmeguntic Lake and Umbagog.

Rebecca still wondered what sort of jaw muscles had made up such words, let alone spoke them in day-to-day fashion without dislocating bones or claudicating tongues. Rebecca had once brought back an old lobster trap which she'd sanded down and refinished. Turned up on its side, it made an interesting table for her apartment. She put a shelf in the center and the fern she'd settled there quickly pressed through the slats in want of more unstructured space.

Michelle Grunsby went to work for the toothpick plant

right out of high school. Though the main office was in Wilton, she was secretary to a production supervisor whose office was in Strong, where the actual physical plant stood. She attended part-time classes at the University of Maine in nearby Farmington.

A Grunsby or two had always worked for the Forster Company as far back as 1888. That was the year after Charles Forster moved the company to Strong. It took a year for Peter Grunsby, then a local farmer's son, to decide that manufacturing the tiny bits of wood was not beneath him after all. The wage was decent and it beat being third in line for his father's land.

Grunsbys had worked for Forster's ever since. If you added it all up, those Grunsbys had turned out about half a light-year's worth of toothpicks. They could've built a tiny bridge to the stars with all those toothpicks. An ant highway to Proxima Centauri, given time. Dauntless and adventurous Formicidae might be sent ahead to colonize, swarthy army ants and Argentine fire ants to squelch any rebellion. Leaf-cutting worker ants could be retrained in technical institutes offering government scholarships and easy loans wherein they would be taught to carry toothpicks to the forward line of the bridge and glue them together with the Elmer's glue-like binding that they would be genetically altered to produce at will from their abdomens. Honeydew ants would be brought along as living food bottles, disgorging their sweet droplets at a steady pace.

A microdot black-and-white glossy of Albert Einstein might be so-glued to the lead ant's thorax and Einstein could sway on this gigabillion toothpick bridge as it tottered in the infinite vacuum of space. The effects on gravity would certainly be tested (he'd always had a weak stomach).

Marie used to stick three toothpicks in each juicy cabbage roll, binding ground beef to steamed green cabbage plucked fresh from her garden, the scent of which used to drive Taft to the kitchen early, as she well knew. Cabbage butterflies skittered when they saw her coming.

Rebecca stuck her long-distance, first-class from Maine, toothpick in her top desk drawer and looked at the phone as if it should be ringing. But stubbornly was not.

"Well," she said aloud. It had been weeks since Michael had gone. She hadn't spoken to him in ages. Often, Rebecca tried to picture him in Florida, lying under palm trees, cracked coconut in hand, probably staring at girls in skimpy bathing suits with exotic floral patterns and tawny, freckled skin, well-oiled and inviting. They were images best left unvisualized.

Rebecca shook herself. Perhaps she should telephone him? There was an awful lot of mail for Michael gathering in an uneasy heap in his mailbox. What better excuse?

Michael, pacing between the kitchen and the living room, picked up the receiver on the third ring. "Hello?" He held the phone to his ear, favoring his neck ever so slightly. Still sensitive. "Hello?" he repeated with no little irritation.

"Hi. Sorry. I guess I didn't hear you the first time or something. I just froze for a second there or something. I don't know what it is really—something."

"Who is this?" asked Michael with emphasis on the who.

"It's me, Rebecca."

"Oh. Hi, Rebecca." Michael settled himself on the edge of the sofa. He waited for her to speak next.

"How are you?"

"Fine."

"How's—" how to put this tactfully, "—everything?"

"Everything's fine. Dad's doing as well as can be expected." He could hear his father now in his bedroom making noises on his concertina.

Sometimes, whether by practice or accident, Taft managed to assemble enough notes so as to almost barely produce a melody of sorts. If you could catch six cats in a narrow hard rock cave and manage to step on all their hairy tails at nearly the precise instant and capture the moment on cheap audiotape and replay it in infinite succession and staccato fashion on a tinny cassette deck with only one abused speaker, you'd begin to understand the rudiments of Taft's concertina stylings.

"How's everything at the university?"

"Okay," answered Rebecca. She went on to describe the past week's conniving and politicking. Then added, "Today's a holiday of sorts."

"Oh?"

"I'm here all alone. The entire department is in a meeting."

Michael didn't know what to say next. He didn't care about any meeting. Was there a point to this telephone call? Besides putting money in the phone company's pocket?

"So, I was cleaning up, you know, keeping busy and I noticed a lot of mail has piled up here for you. I was wondering if maybe you'd like to go over some of it on the telephone. I could tell you what each piece is and you could let me know how to—"

Michael cut her off. "Don't bother, Rebecca. Just toss it all in a box or an envelope or something, would you? Send it on here."

"All right." This was a turn of events she hadn't been expecting. "If that's what you want?"

"Yes. That would be easiest."

"Okay, you're the boss." She gathered her thoughts. "Do you expect to be staying there a while yet?"

Michael nodded for only himself to know. "Yes, it looks like it." He had been unable to convince his father to move out to California with him. It would be the perfect solution. He could go back to his job and his father could stay with him at the apartment. Taft had refused. Refused to go, refused to listen.

The subject had become taboo.

Taft had his own ideas, they'd merely been held up because of Michael's accident.

Michael massaged his temples. His ears were ringing. Sometimes he couldn't tell whether Taft was playing the concertina or if he was merely hearing remnant sound waves rolling around like cold, glassy marbles in his eardrums. He said goodbye to Rebecca and went outdoors to clear his head and his thoughts.

Rebecca numbly bundled up Michael's mail and addressed the large manilla envelope with big, disappointed strokes.

The envelope entered the stream of the afternoon's mail.

Due to extenuating circumstances, that envelope would take nearly nine days to arrive in Brooksville, Florida. And by then it wouldn't matter because too many other streams were moving in too many other directions at once for it to matter one bit.

Rebecca, task completed, stared at the office and down the empty hall which faced out across her desk. It was one of those days. She suspected it was the sun. There must be some sort of physical explanation to explain why some days colors seemed bleached out, less vibrant. The bright red of yesterday was lusterless today. The lemon yellow could barely pass for chiffon. Even the sky seemed more white than blue.

Maybe it was a magnetic condition of light. Some confluence of the sun and a hidden binary companion or a reflection of color that got soaked up by the moon.

Someone should look into the matter.

# 41

Taft had other things to do.

He knew in his heart that this would be the last day that he played the concertina.

He'd barely the energy to play at all. His muscles lay wasted and useless. Walking itself had become a mere movement of his pain-wracked, cancer-ridden bones, rather than an exercise of expanding and contracting muscles. An artifact of dying more than an act of life.

He looked like a thin scarecrow and walked like a stick man. He was reminded of the game, Hang Man, where the object was for the challenger to guess the letters of a word before the stick man could be drawn and hung. He was just about out of guesses.

Oh, he knew he could linger on. Maybe for months. But what would he do in all that time? Lie in a hospital bed hooked up to an IV dripping sugar and morphine? Lie and stare up with dead eyes from his dead body at his son who refused to go home and get on with his life? Let his wife, Marie, get too far ahead of him on the road?

No.

Taft locked the bedroom door. A nearly impossible task that took seemingly Herculean strength these days. He crawled into bed and removed the little plastic bag of pills he'd stashed under the mattress. He had pills he'd swiped from Ellen's house, pills which he'd been prescribed by his doctor, pills which Marie had been prescribed by her doctor and a leftover assortment from the medicine chest in his own house, even some whose expiration dates had passed.

It was fitting.

It was apropos.

He had brought a big glass of water from the kitchen. One by one, Taft swallowed the pills and followed each one with a tiny sip of water. He didn't want to run out of pills before he ran out of water. He was master of his own destiny.

Taft only hoped and prayed all those pills would make it through his plugged insides and stay down long enough to dissolve and, by doing so, dissolve him.

Taft folded the empty plastic bag and let it drop to the floor. He closed his eyes while the rumbling in his stomach became a roar. He dreamed of Marie—as he knew he would.

She stood in the backyard, dressed in her favorite blue shorts, canvas shoes and a white sweatshirt with a caricature of Einstein on the front and a drawing of a chalkboard with a multitude of mathematical symbols and equations on the back. This number over that number. Letters and numbers mixed up together. Taft had never understood how that worked. It was all gobbledygook.

'You Figure It Out' was the caption beneath the blackboard.

You Figure It Out.

Taft called his wife. She looked up for a moment, then went on. She was busy painting the legs of a wooden sofa frame with a wide nylon brush. White paint was everywhere, as if someone had been shooting at the gallon paint can with a .22 caliber rifle. Paint ran up to Marie's elbows and lay in patches on her knees. She held the brush between her thumb and two fingers, working like a pro, using the edge of the bristles. She'd removed the cushions. Freshly washed, the damp cushions were lying outside beside the garage, basking in the sun.

Taft called his wife again. Once more she looked up for a moment and then went back to work. She wanted to finish the sofa before dark. She wanted to get it in the house.

"Need help?"

Marie shook her head. Taft watched, fascinated as the paint literally crept up the legs of the sofa and finally seemed to climb into the air itself. Marie rose and kept on brushing at the air. Thick white globs of painted weighted down the bristles and she twirled the brush all around. The garage, the grass, the driveway, all the trees and the sky itself were getting lost in all that white that came shooting off the brush. The blobs shot like comets streaking past, revealing liquid white tails.

He felt as if he was watching a cartoon. Soon all that was left was the hole where Marie's face (set and grim with duty) painted up the last patch and disappeared. Everything, Everywhere was white. Taft looked at his arms. He looked at his feet. They were gone. All he could see was white.

And that wasn't seeing anything at all.

# 42

Marie was mad.

Nobody told her it would be so lonely.

Nobody told her it would be so boring.

And she never would have even guessed that being dead meant that you had to show up in the dreams of whoever it was who was dreaming about you.

Some of those dreams that her husband Taft had been having, for instance. She hadn't dreamt the old sex pervert still had it in him. If she'd known then, while she was alive, some of the dreams of his that she knew about now, well, their sex life might not have petered out years ago. . .

Aaron Michael on the other hand; suddenly she's in Mexico, chasing around with girls in bikinis and having to listen to Taft's father while she tried to play cribbage (not that he was a bad accordionist).

No, it wasn't easy having to show up in everybody's dreams.

Her girls were always dreaming about her, too. Motherly type dreams. Lots of chores. She seemed to get less rest dead than she had alive.

And this Einstein thing was driving her nuts. She was certain there'd been no pictures of Einstein hanging in any of her houses as she was growing up, or even later for that matter. What was he doing here? His curious eyes seemed to follow her from room to room.

Sleep itself had become next to impossible. She nearly always slept on the floor and occasionally on a sofa. The beds were okay if she were in a frame of mind to want to relive every dream she'd ever dreamt while sleeping in that particular bed, as she had been dismayed to discover. But it wasn't something she was up for everyday by any means. These things had to be taken in small amounts.

Marie saw Taft coming. She was painting that old sofa. She'd discovered it in the garage of her last house, well, next-to-last house. The cushions were a bit mildewed and worn, but the frame was good. Solid. She'd paint it up and scrub the cushions. It was a good length. She'd be able to sleep on the sofa when she was finished. It was long and flat. Maybe she'd leave it out on the street. If she moved it into one of the houses, Marie had no idea what might happen.

If there were laws of physics or otherwise in this place, they weren't written down and they were beyond her comprehension.

Marie felt bad. She really did. About not letting Taft in like that. But she wasn't ready for him yet. So she painted him out. Taft would understand. He would have to. He must follow his own road.

When it was time, the colors would come back, renewed, and the white would dissipate like fog. She'd be with him then.

The old fool. What did he have to go and kill himself for? She still hadn't reconciled her feelings about his keeping his own illness from her. Now this. Sometimes that man was impossible.

# 43

"Michael?"

He opened his eyes into the sun then quickly shut them again. He rolled over onto his belly and pushed himself up. The grass dimpled his arms.

"You okay?"

"Yeah," answered Michael, dusting off his pant legs and squinting in the sun. He looked toward the house. The music had stopped. "How are you, Ellen?"

"Fine." She shifted, embarrassed and nervous. "I just haven't seen you around much, that's all." What she meant was that Michael hadn't taken the initiative and called on her once since their Saturday expedition. "I wanted to say hello and see how you were doing."

"Okay." He followed Ellen's gaze across the backyard. The garden was looking good as ever. "Alex has been coming over every afternoon, keeping Dad company, weeding the garden, watering—"

"I know." Michael seemed indifferent to her presence and once again she wondered why she bothered.

"I hope it's all right."

"Of course it is."

"I hope he's not falling behind in his school work or anything."

Ellen shook her head. Her hair lifted in the breeze sweeping past their faces. "No. Alex does great in school. Can you imagine? He actually looks forward to homework."

Michael laughed.

"How's Taft?"

Michael shrugged wearily. "Okay, I guess. You can't

imagine how hard it is to see him wasting away like this." He stuffed his hands in his pockets. "I mean, Dad and I never really got along, you know."

She nodded.

"I don't know why. He was a good father, I suppose. We just couldn't communicate with each other. Even as a boy. I just didn't feel that I could talk to him." He looked at Ellen, the house and finally his shoes. "I don't know," he said slowly, "maybe it was my fault—" His voice trailed off.

Ellen reached out and took Michael's hand. "It's no one's fault," she said. She knew it was a pat thing to say. But what else could she say? "He loves you and I know you love him. Everything else is just debris, the stuff that we clutter our lives with."

Michael bit his cheek. His mouth began to form words but he didn't know what they would be. He pulled his hand back from Ellen's grip.

Ellen teetered. "I think I'll go see how Taft is doing," she said with calm reserve.

Michael shut his eyes and let out a lugubrious sigh. He knew he was shutting Ellen out and that it was hurting her, but what could he do? His hands became fists in his pockets.

# 44

Ellen went in through the unlocked kitchen door and made her way over familiar territory to Taft's bedroom. The door was closed. She put an ear to the warm plywood and heard nothing. He was probably asleep.

She might just peep in on him and see how he looked. Ellen gripped the knob and meant to turn it slowly but the knob wouldn't budge at all. It seemed to be locked from the inside. Ellen almost called Michael then decided against it.

She knocked lightly, the rapping echoed loudly in the empty hallway. "Taft?" she whispered. Pause. "Hello? It's me, Ellen."

Ellen pressed her ear to the door once more and was rewarded only with the sound of the blood rushing around in her ears. "Taft?" she called, a notch higher on the decibel scale.

Sensing doom, she quickly went in search of Michael. She found him exactly where she'd left him, standing with his feet planted in the grass as unmoving as a eucalyptus tree. "Michael," she said, her breathing was coming faster now.

He turned. "What is it?"

"Your dad doesn't answer when I knock and his door's locked."

"He might be asleep. I mean, he can't go anywhere. He's all but bedridden now and is hooked up to that miserable IV virtually all the time."

"Michael, I'm worried. . .and scared. I have a bad feeling."

Michael looked away, not wanting to comprehend her fear. "He was playing his concertina not an hour ago—"

"Please, Michael."

Michael nodded and led the way into the house. "This is

154

silly."

"I didn't hear anything at all," explained Ellen. "I couldn't even hear him breathing."

"That doesn't mean anything. You'd not likely hear him through the door." Michael knocked loudly. "Dad, wake up. You've got the door locked." He rattled the knob. "Dad, come on, open up!"

He rattled the knob again. "Maybe he's too weak to walk."

"Can you open it?"

"Sure," said Michael, eyeballing the simple lock. "Have you got a hairpin or something?"

Ellen shook her head.

"Be right back," said Michael. He ran to the kitchen pantry where his father kept a small household tool box and returned with a tiny screwdriver, one made for eyeglasses repair.

He stuck the end of the screwdriver into the hole in the rim of the doorknob and pushed. "Nothing's happening. I don't understand. I thought they were supposed to open this way." He looked at Ellen as if she had the answer.

"Don't look at me." Ellen's face was the color and complexion of white pastry flour. "Do something, Michael."

Michael's hand trembled as he tried the lock again. "I'll have to break it," he said with finality. He slammed his weight into the door and heard a cracking noise, but wasn't sure if it was the door, the door frame or his shoulder to blame for it. The door held.

"Wait," said Ellen, before Michael could throw himself at the door again. "Let's do it together. Maybe with both our weight —"

Michael nodded. "On three," he said. "One, two, three!"

They charged and the door exploded with a crack of plywood. The door frame splintered and the door moved forward, the upper hinge separated from the wall, and the door dangled dangerously. Paint chips sprinkled the floor.

Michael held the door up for Ellen to get through. "Careful," he said, bits of wood stuck out like jagged spears and finishing nails bent menacingly outwards.

Standing in in the room, they stared.

Taft lay in bed. The IV was still dripping. He looked all right, if a little pallid, like a bit of white asparagus. Michael was amazed that his dad hadn't been wakened by the breaking door.

Ellen touched Taft's forehead. She shuddered and tried to hide it. She clutched her arms to steady herself.

Taft was cold.

Ellen was, too. "I'm sorry, Michael," she whispered. The words spilled out her mouth from the depths of her soul.

# 45

The house didn't appear the same.

It looked dead. The door was locked, the curtains drawn. The St. Augustine grass seemed to be standing still, as if in cryogenic suspension. Alex stood on the sidewalk straddling his bicycle, looking lost. Cora, Mary and Elizabeth crowded into the car with Michael. Cora was driving.

Ellen was nowhere to be found. She could not understand why Michael was constantly pushing himself away from her. And ever since Taft died, he'd all but refused to see her or even speak with her. It was as if he needed someone to blame for his father's death and he'd decided it would be her. Whenever she tried to speak with him, he got angry with her and finally she'd decided it was entirely too much effort to make any more overtures of peace or friendship. She couldn't let him treat her like that any longer.

Dr. Johnston had been called. He signed the death certificate. Death by natural causes. What would be the point of implying anything different?

Cora, Mary and Elizabeth had flown down at once, together in a clump, like a remnant from a flock of birds who'd unwisely waited until the last moment to fly south. They'd taken charge of everything. Taft's body was already in Michigan or would be soon.

Michael insisted on driving up alone, like he had a scant couple of weeks earlier with his father, but his sisters beat up on him until he was forced to agree to one of his sister's accompanying him. That would be Cora. Elizabeth had the girls. Mary had her teaching job. It was easiest for Cora to arrange the time. Michael sat next to her in the car.

Michael didn't talk. He didn't so much as look back as the house disappeared from sight. He never could have admitted to anyone, especially his family (now reduced by two), what he was thinking, what he felt inside.

Michael hated his father. All his life his father and he had not been able to be friends. Now, just when the barriers were beginning to come down and they were making some progress, beginning to understand one another, his father goes and does this thing. They might have been friends after all. And not merely loved each other as father and son are bound to do.

His father killed himself. It was as if he'd run away. He'd run away from Michael like he didn't care.

That was how Michael felt.

He felt as if he'd finally tried to get close to his father and when he did, his father chose to run away.

He hated him for that.

At the airport, Michael sat in one of the blue, molded plastic seats in a row beside the big window. People pressed all around. The stink of cigarette smoke and chewing gum fouled the air. He looked glumly out the window, watching the baggage handlers load the plane in the rain. It was one of those days where it was going to drizzle gray rain unceasingly. It was a boring type of rain. If only it would storm. Some thunder, some lightning, that was what was called for. Give it some sizzle. Some pizazz.

The workers' blue uniforms were barely visible except for their collars, beneath orange raingear. He kept expecting to see the men carrying out his father in a casket on one of those electric carts they manipulated. Would they lift his father's body into the casket three on a side like pallbearers or merely toss him in like an oversized piece of luggage?

When Elizabeth and Mary departed, he numbly said goodbye. They hugged him in turn and he weakly responded. He wasn't used to hugging his sisters or being hugged back. His mother was the only person who really knew how to hug him.

He turned on his heels and started walking back to the

parking lot without even looking to see if his sister Cora was following him.

"Wait up!" called Cora. Her purse bounced against her side as she tried to match stride with her stupid younger brother.

Michael kept going.

Cora managed to catch him when he'd gotten stalled behind a slow-moving mass of visitors from Montreal. She struck him across the chest with her purse, not with intent to do bodily harm, but viciously nevertheless, like only a sister could do.

"Ow, hey!" complained Michael.

"You deserve it," Cora said. French-speaking heads turned. Cora nearly cussed them out for curiousness, yet held her tongue. Detroit was not far from Canada and she knew the French language well. The picturesque expression '*Va te faire foutre*' came to mind.

Michael said nothing.

"Really, Michael," said Cora. "You've got to stop carrying on so."

"I don't know what you're talking about," he lied. "I'm fine."

Cora nearly flung him over the escalator. Love-thy-brother love could take many forms. Right now it was shaped like a fine-edged axe. "We're all suffering."

Michael stared forward. Hating everyone.

"How do you think I feel? How do you think we all feel?" She wanted to sympathize with her brother, but she was having a difficult enough time coping herself.

"He's such an idiot."

Cora's expression changed sharply from fatigued and strained to quizzical. "Who?"

Michael scowled. He cocked his jaw toward the ceiling. They were fast approaching the bottom of the escalator and Michael tripped on the landing and skidded forward. Cora followed.

"Michael," she said. "Who? Who is an idiot?"

He turned on her so fast that it frightened her, his face a hideous alter ego. She was afraid he was going to reach out and grab her shoulders and fling her across the room. He didn't. He didn't touch her.

"Him!" he spat venomously.

"Him who? You're not making sense!" She was nearly crying now.

"Dad. Good old Dad Dad." Michael's words came out like toxin. "Good old Dad Dad ups and leaves us. Couldn't wait to go, could he?" Michael said savagely. "Barely put Mother in the ground and, whoops, off he goes!"

The tears were unstoppable now. Cora didn't even try to slow them. "He was dying, Michael. He was in pain you couldn't imagine." She fought to reason with him. Twenty people stopped in their tracks and stared, and listened.

"He was alive!" screamed Michael. "He was alive!" Michael's face was the color of cooked eggplant one second, then pale as wet flour the next. Changing colors like a mutating mold or exogalactic virus. "Every minute he was here he was alive. Now he's dead. When you're gone, you're gone! How the fuck could he do that? That stupid son of a bitch. First Mother, then him. How dare he? HOW DARE HE!"

Cora reeled. She'd never in her life heard her brother raise his voice like this. Michael ran ahead, pushing heedlessly past the prying travelers who preferred this spontaneous family drama to watching the uneventful arrivals and departures of various commercial jetliners.

Cora stumbled and made her way to the nearest ladies room. "Are you all right?" asked some nameless, faceless figure. Cora merely murmured and hurried on. She stood in the corner of the farthest stall and wept uncontrollably.

Nearly forty minutes later she returned to her father's car in the short-term parking garage. Michael was leaning against the passenger side door, his back to her. She said nothing. She climbed inside and leaned over to unlock his door. Michael got in without hesitation and said nothing in return.

It was dark by the time they left the airport. Cora didn't feel like driving on. They spent the night at a high-rise hotel at the airport perimeter, taking separate rooms. Cora went down to dinner and Michael stayed in his room. She didn't invite his company and he wouldn't have given it.

# 46

"Stop!" commanded Michael.

"What is it?" Cora slowed down. The background seemed to catch up to them. They were in Georgia now and it was unseasonably warm.

"There," said Michael. He stuck his arm out the open window.

"What?" She saw nothing but a near-derelict gas station.

"That's it." Michael made the announcement as if his sister was supposed to have even the slightest idea what in the world he was talking about. He'd been vague and barely rational and only seemed to be getting worse as each day, each hour passed.

"That's what?" She'd stopped the car along the shoulder of the highway. Gravel and sand scrunched beneath the tires. A grasshopper complained loudly. She looked out the window toward the gas station. Except for the sound of passing cars they could have been on the moon.

"That's where we stopped," explained Michael.

Cora backed up the car and headed up the service drive. She pulled in front of the red pumps. They could have used a coat of fresh paint. The smell of gasoline overwhelmed all scent of the otherwise vegetative countryside.

"What are you doing?" asked Michael.

"May as well get some gas."

Michael watched the station attendant as he poked around under the hood of an old Chevy. "Dad got sick and threw up all over himself. Right here." He paused.

The worker opened the door of the Chevy and tried the engine. The starter whirred and the engine refused to turn over.

"I remember he wanted to drive. Then he got sick and we

pulled. I remember that attendant," he said to Cora, and pointed at the slouch-backed mechanic who'd taken a crescent wrench to the carburetor. "I yelled at him."

"You yelled at him? What for?"

"For being sick."

"Oh, you mean Dad. I thought you meant the service guy."

"No."

Cora filled the car with gas and paid off the attendant who accepted her money silently and with engine-greased hands.

"Good luck," the attendant said, turning back to his carburetor job.

"Thanks," replied Cora, though she did not know what for.

Michael never budged from the car.

# 47

Michigan had pulled itself in and curled up for the winter. Trees shook themselves of excess and storm windows replaced summer screens. Frost seemed to spring from the earth. The lakes and rivers swelled and slowed. Enterprising squirrels bought up stocks of acorn butter and traded in acorn futures.

Mechanical-minded men checked the fluid in their radiators, topping off the slender tanks with antifreeze, maybe adjusted the points on their carburetors for good measure while they were there. While inside, their wives pulled great gobs of sweaters from cedar chests and put away their summer dresses and shoes.

Trout grew torpid and wrapped seaweed mufflers tightly round their gills. The Great Grandmother of All Trout had taught them the craft of fashioning them from aqueous weeds and cloth debris tossed or lost in the lakes. The Great Grandmother of All Trout had a shiny pronged hook embedded in her jaw which protruded outward. She had captured it many seasons before in Lake Michigan. A hapless amateur fisherman had cast his line near her lair where she waited.

She'd heard about the shiny hooks of death and was determined to own one for her own uses. She'd dashed for the hook the minute it stopped its descent into the forbidding black waters. Like the mighty Nimrod himself, she tossed the pin of death into her mouth and tugged with all her brawn. The stunned fisherman let burst a guttural cry and pulled back stubbornly, his feet braced against the sides of his fiberglass fishing boat.

The Great Grandmother of All Trout prevailed (her need was greater). The line snapped and the jolted fisherman fell against the rim of the boat, bruising his upper back and neck. He cursed and tossed the pole against the hull. The Great Grandmother of All Trout, Katrina, raced homeward with her catch, her prize.

All members of the Trout Court gathered round as she displayed the near magical fishhook. "With this," Katrina proclaimed, "we shall improve our lot." The Great Grandmother of All Trout promptly started experiments and discussions with her closest advisors to determine how this sharp-edged steel instrument could best suit their purposes and needs. Information theorists were contacted to perform independent outside studies.

The Great Grandmother of All Trout took up knitting in her spare time, using the hook now firmly bedded in her chin as deftly as a naturally-born appendage. Her quilts and comforters were legendary. And her mufflers, of course, with winter coming on, were quite popular.

Further expeditions were sent out, volunteers appeared. It was their duty, their desire, to seek out further hooks. Many returned. Some bloodied and torn, with and without the much-valued hooks. Many did not. These were mourned.

# 48

The Grand Haven Cemetery hadn't changed much since his last visit. Oh, there were one or two more souls propped into place. The leaves had danced around. And the rain had stopped. Not much else was new. Off in the distance sat a gravesite surrounded by flowers. A new neighbor.

Michael sat in his usual spot in his father's car. Cora wasn't driving though. Her husband, Troy, drove. Cora sat stiffly in the backseat with Mary. Theirs was one of the first cars to arrive. Taft had arrived early. It was Indian Summer. Seventy-five degrees. If the tombstones had been made of snow, they'd have melted into the ground by now and seeped down below the crust and into the core of the Earth. Was the center of the Earth packed with the bodies, the souls of the dead? Did their remains ooze down beneath the mantle through the weight of gravity and the push of rain?

Michael toyed with his tie. Troy stopped the car at the end of the cul-de-sac and shut off the engine. Nobody said a word. It was as if they'd already gone through the entire vocabulary and there just wasn't anything left to say. They'd have to wait until somebody made up some new words, maybe some new concepts and put them out in book form.

Michael opened his door and put his feet to the pavement. His muscles felt stiff. He had the oddest sensation, for only a moment, that he'd felt something, a vibration, a sensation of the past leaking up from the ground through the soles of his shoes, then his feet and into his knees and directly from there to his brain. He straightened and waited for his sisters to climb out from the backseat.

Everybody looked two hundred years old. He closed the car

door but didn't lock it. Pretty safe place to park a car, a cemetery was.

"Imagine if Dad's brother had lived, if he was here," said Mary.

"Ernest?" said Troy.

"No, the other one," said Mary, shaking her head.

Michael stopped dead in his tracks. A cemetery was as good a place as any to do it. "What other one?" he asked with a voice of doom.

"The twin."

"Dad had a twin brother?"

"Yes, he—"

"Mary," said Cora, "I don't think we should talk about it, not now."

"I only thought how odd it would be to see someone here who looked like Dad, I mean, while we're here burying Dad."

Michael tipped to one side and caught himself by clutching the hood of a car. His father had had a twin brother? Did everyone but him know this as well? "When did he die?"

"At childbirth," said Cora. "Drop it."

Troy handed his wife the car keys. "They jab my legs and I don't want to poke a hole in my suit," he said, shifting ground. "Could you put them in your purse?"

Cora whispered yes. She and Mary held hands. It seemed to help. With her free hand Cora wrestled with her small leather purse and the car keys. It wasn't working.

"I'll take them," Michael offered, his words a susurrant vibration in the open air. *Trust me*, whispered the wind.

"Thanks," said Cora, unthinkingly. She handed the keyring to Michael who stopped and made a show of searching for an adequate pocket.

The others went on ahead. Michael turned, making it appear nonchalant and tapping his pockets as if he'd left something in the car, he headed in the reverse direction. His steady steps quickened until he found himself running the remaining distance to Taft's well-cared for Oldsmobile (Ransom

Olds would have been pleased with the attention Taft had given the car while he lived).

The keys jangled in Michael's pants pocket. He threw open the door and grasped the wheel with one hand while digging into his pocket for the ignition key with the other. He found it quickly enough and twisted the starter with a snap. The engine roared as his foot inadvertently hit the accelerator.

Michael spun the car round the cul-de-sac and hit the main road with a bump that might have torn loose the transmission or at least busted the oil pan. Oncoming traffic pressed him in both directions. Cars honked but he didn't hear them.

Elizabeth, standing over her mother and father's grave, watched in horror as her brother ran off across the lawn and stole the family car.

She wanted to scream.

Had Grand Haven Cemetery of St. Clair Shores been a supermarket parking lot and not a cemetery, a place of the dead, she might have. She might have screamed and never stopped.

# 49

The Interstate became a downhill bobsled run, like the one at Mount Van Hoevenburg, a twisted glass smooth mile and a half of treachery. The Oldsmobile shook like a sleek one-piece, brakeless bobsled taking curves and bumps without undue complaint.

Michael stopped only for three things. Gas, bathrooms and coffee.

Sixteen hours later he was in Brooksville, the Oldsmobile wheezing and steaming like the last mule in the Grand Canyon, forced to keep up with the flow of tourists whose only desire was to be carried to the bottom of the canyon just so they could be carried back up again. The Rio Grande a mere distraction. Something to do. Someplace to say they'd been. Something to take snapshots of.

Michael didn't bother to put up the windows and he didn't think to shut the car door. He ran to the front of the house. Dark empty walls and windows faced him. Suddenly he was afraid of ghosts. Would his mother's and father's ghosts haunt him here? Or in Michigan? They were buried in Michigan. But they'd both died here, in Brooksville. Where would they go? His hands shook, 132 ounces of coffee and 1350 milligrams of caffeine on an empty stomach and no sleep (not to mention waxing psychosis) could have that effect on anyone.

Abruptly, Michael found himself needing to pee (maybe it was all that shaking). Desperately. He went to open the front door and remembered that he'd left the keys in the ignition. Trembling, he ran to the edge of the front porch and leaned into the big shrub. It was two in the morning, who would notice?

Feeling calmer, he walked back to his father's car and

removed the keys. He glanced up and down the street. No lights were visible in the windows, only streetlights and the occasional porch light stood out.

None too sure of himself, he unlocked the front door of his parents' house and pushed it open. His ears twitched. What was that he'd heard? He held his breath and listened. Nothing.

He was going crazy.

That was okay. The first step to recovery was knowing that you had a problem.

He coughed. Loudly. "Hrrrmme, rhemesm," he said. He pricked up his ears and listened. Still nothing. He struggled for the light switch beside the front door and managed to turn on the outside porch light. Yellow bug light lit the front of the house and some of it sneaked inside the living room. It was enough to see by.

The room was quiet. Deathly quiet.

Michael searched every room in the house. And he left every light on.

He wouldn't remember going to bed or deciding to sleep, but in the morning, he woke to discover himself lying on the living room floor, fully dressed (one shoelace had come untied), lamps still blazing though their illumination was blanched and overwhelmed by the incoming sunlight.

The front door hung open. The room felt cold and all his bones and even several of his internal organs were stiff. He willfully opened his eyelids and stared into blue nylon carpeting. The pressure in his bladder was exquisite. If he had the strength he'd go to the bathroom.

Silvery-winged insects, moths, mosquitoes, and no-see-ums filled the house. The neighbor's calico cat had come and gone, leaving a dark stain on the wall near the door.

"Michael?" He rolled onto his elbows as Ellen stepped into the room. "Michael, are you all right?"

"Yes," he groaned sleepily. "Hi." He waved halfheartedly. His mouth felt, tasted and smelled like a bog. His brain swelled like a giant sphagnum moss sponge. The American Indians had used the sphagnum as a natural diaper. Maybe American consumers should return to the custom. It might solve or at least reduce the landfill problem.

Besides, Michael pitied the poor archaeologists of the future who would have to sort through all those dung- and urine-soaked specimens. Archaeology was losing its romance. No more exotic jungles and even more exotic pottery. Tomorrow's archaeologists would be sifting through Huggies and Styrofoam coffee cups and costume jewelry.

Ellen flipped off the outside light. It barely made a difference in the quality of color. "Alex told me he saw you lying on the floor in here."

"Oh."

"You scared him. He came running in and shouting for me to telephone the police."

Michael sat on the floor, his arms locked round his knees. He was dying of thirst and had desperately to pee again. He shut his eyes as Ellen continued talking.

"He thought you'd been murdered or something. Can you imagine?" Ellen went on, watching Michael intently. His face was pale and swollen. He was dirty and looked discombobulated. His suit of clothes was rumpled and stunk. "Alex saw your father's car in the driveway, and the door was open and the front door to the house was open and then he saw you on the floor and, well—"

She'd run out of steam.

Ellen had never been one for soliloquy. She didn't even talk to herself out loud, alone, like many people did. A stubborn, discomfiting silence followed. "Well, if you're all right—"

Michael nodded without bothering to raise his head or open his eyes.

"Okay then. If there's anything you need, or if you want to talk or anything," she said valiantly, "you know where to find me."

Nothing. Not even a shake of his head that time.

"Okay then. Bye."

Michael listened for her footsteps across the porch. When their sound faded, he let out a loud, melancholic sigh. The house seemed to join him. It was a sing-a-long sigh. It was a sing-a-long day.

He struggled to his feet and promptly fell face forward towards the floor. Fortunately for him he'd managed the motor skills to put his arms out in front of himself and saved his face from total destruction.

On the second attempt, he did better. He not only managed to stand, he managed to walk, though his gait was unsteady and he had the jitters. Michael hobbled to the bathroom and relieved himself. He thought about coffee. He could've used a cup just then but he didn't have the strength to manage it. Grinding the beans, finding a cup, measuring out the water. It all seemed like too much effort.

The best he could manage was to cup his stiff fingers beneath the water faucet of the bathroom sink and sip water from his leaking hands. The water came out room temperature and only served to turn the goop in his mouth to gunk. He wiped his lips with the side of his palm.

Back in the living room, he shut the front door and locked it. Ellen had left it open when she'd gone. She was probably mad. He shrugged indifferently. That wasn't his fault, after all.

Out the window, he saw the Oldsmobile damp with morning condensation. The car door stood gaping like a broken gull's wing. The battery was most likely dead. He turned his back on it and considered the house.

A dream from the night before came sweeping back into his field of vision. The family gathered in a townhouse that one of his sisters bought. They talked about Uncle Jerome. Someone said that the last time Uncle Jerome came he brought his wife and all five of his children. They'd stayed all together in the narrow, one bedroom, two level townhouse and all the other residents in the building had been angry that he'd imposed such a large brood upon them. His uncle had even had a hole torn in the back wall so he could get his big Harley Davidson motorcycle inside out of the elements. Everybody laughed at the memory.

Then, his sister, Elizabeth, had come downstairs leading their father by a flaccid, nearly bloodless hand. Taft stopped on the landing at the midpoint of the stairway and stood sagging against the wall. His eyes opened and closed. He didn't recognize Michael. Once though, he'd looked Michael's way and smiled.

That had made Michael feel better. Michael had the sickening sense that his father didn't know, really didn't know, if he was alive or if he was dead. He just kept opening and closing his eyes. And no one knew what he saw.

That was all of the dream that Michael could remember.

# 50

The telephone rang once. Before it could let loose a second chirrup, Michael unplugged it with methodical precision and tossed it out the front door. The device crashed to the lawn and lay there like a totem. The receiver stayed attached to the dialer by its umbilicus-like cord. The telephone, splayed and useless on the turf, was a symbol. Don't call me, it said.

Michael went out to the garden. The garden was in great shape. Little Alex was doing a hell of a job. Michael glanced back at the house and thought he saw shadows moving in the windows. He stole up beneath them and jumped up quickly. But there was no one inside. No one behind those window panes.

Michael knew then what he had to do. He found the kerosene on a shelf in the kitchen, not in the garage where any rational person would have kept it but out in the kitchen. His father had only used the stuff to light the outdoor barbecue, so what the hell was it doing in the house?

Michael had no time to consider the matter beyond his annoyance. It had taken up nearly an hour of his time to find the pint-sized can as it was. He was losing valuable minutes.

Michael took the can, along with the matches. These he'd found quickly in the kitchen junk drawer. Some of that junk, Michael was confident, had been in the junk drawer of the first kitchen of his childhood recollections and some of those rubber bands were definitely pre-World War I, and headed to Taft and Marie's room.

The bed sat there on its four wobbly legs. Unsteady. Unmade. It still showed the wrinkles. The wrinkles that the depression and movement of his father's body had made before and after he'd died. Maybe some of those wrinkles were even his mother's. Michael couldn't recall his father having washed the sheets the entire time Michael had been in Florida. So they could have been. They could have been his mother's wrinkles as well as his father's. It could have been both of their wrinkles commingled.

The room smelled damp and stale.

Michael poured the kerosene out in lines streaking unevenly across the mattress and bedclothes. He stopped pouring when the kerosene ran out. He carefully, with the tip of his thumbnail, cut a match from the matchbook and lit it.

Standing so close to his mother and father's bed that his trousers touched, he leaned forward with the flame and dropped it from less than twelve inches away.

He heard a whoosh as oxygen burned and left the room. A sudden and stunning wave of heat swept Michael back from the bed (saving his catching fire through no insight of his own) and sent him nearly to the still hanging by broken hinges door.

Acrid smoke filled the room. Michael retreated. Things hadn't gone to plan. But at least he'd killed the bed.

It was Taft and Marie's next-door neighbor who'd spotted the smoke and called the fire department who in turn notified the police.

Marie was horrified. "Aaron Michael! Aaron Michael! What are you doing? Be careful or you'll burn the house down!" she shouted in dismay.

Michael turned in the direction of his mother's voice but couldn't see anything. He couldn't find her through all that smoke. When she burst through the brume of burning sheets and feathers, mattress and kerosene, it was Ellen's face not Marie's that she wore.

"Michael!" she shouted. "What the devil are you doing? You'll burn the house down!"

Michael's face wore a mask of surprise and shock, fear and anger and perhaps, madness. "Watch out," he said. "The bed's on fire."

"What?" Ellen looked from Michael to the flames coming

in orange and yellow light from the open bedroom.

"Get the garden hose!" Ellen yelled in terror as she went off in search of a fire extinguisher. She remembered seeing one bracketed to the wall beside the door between the kitchen and the garage. She grabbed it and ran to the bedroom.

Michael still wasn't back with the garden hose. The next-door neighbor woman, Paula Browner, was yelling out by the front door. "I called the fire department," she snapped with a voice harsher than sandpaper and squeakier than fake fingernails on a chalkboard.

Ellen aimed the fire extinguisher at the bedroom door and shot flame retardant foam in front of her like a shield of ooze shot from an ooze gun in a science fiction flick. The house shook on its foundation, the sirens were that loud.

"Fire Department's here!" announced Paula, still hovering at the front door, afraid to come closer.

"Where's Michael?" called Ellen just as Michael ran into the house, the green garden hose dangling limp in his hand.

"Here."

"You didn't turn it on." Ellen squeezed her face between her hands. "There's no water, Michael. You didn't turn the water on." She repeated the words slowly. Michael didn't seem to understand.

A swarthy and stout fireman in full regalia, brandishing his axe in gloved hands came bounding through the living room door and setting the neighbor, Paula, aside. "Out of the way!" he shouted. "Get out to the street!"

Paula muttered and sputtered and well-I-nevered all the way outside.

"You, too." the firefighter instructed. "The both of you!"

Ellen and Michael hurried out past the line of firemen and fire hoses. They, along with neighbors far and wide, watched from the sidewalk across the street. There hadn't been a show this good since the Fourth of July.

As quickly as it had started, it was over. The neighborhood was quiet as a tomb. Only the children hung about, watching with bright curious eyes as the firemen doffed their gear and rewound their hoses, wiped their faces with clean white handkerchiefs.

Ellen apprised the situation with emotionless eyes. Water soaked everything. The scent of burnt mattress incense was an odor that would linger the day. The house still stood. The fire captain talked to Michael up by the porch. It could have been worse.

She crossed over the street to the two men.

The captain demanded explanations. Michael wasn't good at offering any.

"Hi," said Ellen. "I'm Ellen Pasternak." The fireman gave her a passing nod. "I live up the street."

"I'm kinda busy right now, lady."

"Michael?"

"It's okay," Michael said.

"Would you please come inside, sir. I'd like to go over the incident with you. Please, be careful," the captain said. "There's been some serious damage."

Michael stepped up the porch and into the house ahead of the captain. His name was Jannett and he'd been in Brooksville for eighteen years and a fireman all the while.

Ellen, unasked and uninvited, followed behind.

The living room looked more like it had been visited by a tornado than a fire. Knick-knacks had been knocked to the floor and the sofa had managed to end up on its side. The smell of smoke was near choking inside. The hallway walls were scorched black. "Started inside the house, did it?" said the captain.

Michael nodded.

"What?" said the captain who wasn't looking his way.

"Yes," agreed Michael. "It started in here." There were dark smudges around Michael's eyes like double shiners.

Ellen's feet crunched over broken glass and timber.

Captain Jannett scowled at her. "Careful, young lady. Mind, you oughtn't be here."

"But—" she stammered. "I can help. I mean, well. . ."

The captain reconsidered her. "What do you mean?" he asked evenly.

"You see," Ellen began slowly, rubbing her soot-and foam-caked hands across the sides of her jeans. "I-Michael and I were going to barbecue and then the kerosene was in here and some candles and I guess his father used to keep a lamp in the bedroom and then we fell and he was holding the match and—" She shrugged coyly.

"Ohh," said the captain, a married man himself, though to his sorrow unused to such antics as those the young woman was suggesting. "So." He swiveled about the room, hands on hips. His mouth turned up at the corner like an indicator or a fireman's barometer. "Not much damage." Jannett laughed. "Talk about setting the sheets on fire." He slapped Michael on the shoulder.

Ellen smiled shyly. Michael appeared confused.

"Other than that," said Jannett, "nothing major. Mostly smoke damage."

Not to mention the damage the fire fighters had left, a thought which Ellen diplomatically kept to herself.

The captain turned to Ellen and Michael. "I guess I've got enough for my report." He could see nothing to gain by making trouble for those two. He turned to go and noticed the busted bedroom door.

"That was broken before," put in Michael.

The captain cocked a tickled eyebrow. "My-my," he said. His heavy boots made soggy impressions in the blackened hall carpets as he departed.

If the bed hadn't been reduced to a puddle of molten springs and desiccated, toasted fabric, Ellen would have collapsed right on it. Right then and right there.

# 51

December twenty-third.

Not that you could tell. I mean, Florida was still green, always was, always will be. If they lock all the doors and don't let any new people in.

Come to think of it, figured Michael, there were so many golf courses in Florida already, maybe they should stick up a gate with a chubby guard in a blue uniform. They could call it the Florida State Country Club.

Have a big sign: Members Only.

Palm trees swaying in balmy breezes. All the snowmen are cardboard and plastic and have red electric noses. The Christmas trees have all been cut from Maine forests and stand wrapped in chicken wire like frozen corpses from some macabre concentration camp. The only snow you can find comes in a spray can. Shake-shake, whoosh in your face, Merry Christmas!

Michael stepped out the door and squinted. It was good to be out. He'd never liked being cooped up. And, current events notwithstanding, he'd never been one for hospitals. His sisters had pushed him into checking himself in.

Ostensibly, he'd been in the hospital recovering from shock, superficial burns and smoke inhalation. He and everybody else knew that he'd really been in the hospital because he'd needed the rest. He'd lost his mind or, at the very least, misplaced it.

December twenty-third. His father's birthday. Do dead fathers still have birthdays? It had also been his great-grandfather's birthday. Michael's great-grandfather had been born at the hour of 10:01 PM. Taft came to the world at 10:02 PM. But for a fluke of years they'd have been born a minute apart.

179

Michael took a deep breath. It was the first un-air conditioned lung-full that he'd had in a week. The glare and heat ricocheting off the cars in the visitors parking lot was discomfiting. He was at odds. School was out. His mother and father were dead. Now what?

His feet for the first time in his life seemed directionless.

Michael shuffled off to the right, following the sidewalk as it curved in a gentle arc around the front of the hospital. He knew he'd find Taft's car out there somewhere, with the keys in it. It was the only favor he'd asked of Ellen.

"Please leave Dad's car with the keys in it on the twenty-third," he'd asked.

Ellen, none too thrilled with leaving a car in a busy parking lot with the keys dangling like a dare to the underworld, did, with hesitation, as she'd been asked. She couldn't help but care about Michael even though he made it clear he cared nothing for her.

With little trouble, Michael found Taft's car. She'd rolled up the windows but left the doors unlocked. He opened the windows on each side before getting in. Heat like that contained in a dragon's belly belched out.

Michael got in, adjusted the seat a little closer to the gears, a little straighter in the back, and started the engine. The engine came to life as engines always do when we give them half a chance.

There was no doubt. Michael knew exactly what he would do next. He knew exactly where he was going.

He was going back to the house.

He was going to finish what he'd begun.

The house didn't look as bad as Michael had expected. Not that he knew what to expect. The house wasn't a burnt-out shell. There were no craters in the yard. The car stalled and ran out of gas heading up the drive. Michael got out and tried pushing the backend up out of the street but the car was too heavy and the angle too steep. All he got for his efforts was a thick coat of perspiration and a strained lumbar spine.

Michael was getting mad all over again, though he told himself he wouldn't. Couldn't.

Michael felt the neighbors staring at him from behind their chintz and balloon curtains. Big deal, he thought. Tire tracks tracked across the front lawn where one of the big fire trucks had crouched like a water-spewing alien spacecraft. Soot layered the front porch and stained the wood and cement in gray and black blotches. Black boot prints ran in and out.

Inside, the house was every bit as bad as he'd expected. Furniture overturned, smoke smells in everything and Taft and Marie's bedroom looked like something or someone had set off an incendiary device smack in the middle of it.

Come to think of it, someone had.

That stupid bedroom door still hung by its lone hinge. Michael kicked it savagely. It swung and yawed but stayed put. He gathered up his strength and kicked again. All he could hear was the damn door laughing at him. If only he'd had an axe.

What remained of the garden appeared in good shape. The weeds had been kept at bay. Alex was still doing his job and doing it well. Frost had come and some of the flowers hadn't survived. Alex had put plastic over some of the others.

A giant red sleigh led by a team seven reindeer, with Santa Claus trailing and waving his big mittened hands topped the roof of the house behind. Up and down the street, neighbors decorated their houses with Christmas paraphernalia, colored lights, white lights, nativities, snowmen, angels and Santa Clauses. Myriad stars and trees sprinkled the lawns. Someone had even put green light bulbs in their outside light fixtures. What would the bugs think now? Would they know it was Christmas?

Taft and Marie's house appeared barren and neglected by comparison.

Not a light shone. Not a wreath on the front door. The bug light had burned out nights before.

Maybe he should get a tree? He'd passed a tree lot with a few left down the road a ways. Yes, maybe that would be a good idea. After all, the Christmas tree was supposed to be a symbol for Paradise.

On my way to Paradise.

Michael headed for the car and then remembered that he was out of gas. There was no way he could walk all the way to the tree lot and then back again carrying a Frasier fir or a big Scotch pine on his back.

Michael paused and considered. Maybe he'd find some gasoline in the garage. A quick search told him there was. In a slightly battered and very rusted out can beside the old lawn mower remained a half gallon of gasoline. He had two choices now. Two clear choices that he could see. Number one, he could pour this gasoline in a ring around the living room and burn the house down or, number two, he could pour what little gas there was into the Oldsmobile. And get a Christmas tree.

It took him a second, but Michael decided on the Christmas tree. Like a burr that had gotten stuck in his mind, the tree had suddenly possessed him.

Michael arrived at the Christmas tree lot and picked out what to him appeared to be the best of the remaining trees. The man running the lot, dressed in soiled brown jeans and a red-and-white flannel shirt which was decidedly too warm for Florida's climate, helped him tie the tree down. They'd managed to get it halfway in the trunk. There were going to be a hell of a lot of needles to clean out afterwards. Michael thanked the man, paid him twenty-two dollars and drove off.

Michael untied the rope and set the tree down on the side of the house. He didn't think anyone would bother it there. He knew of a hardware store in town. Needing some other things too, he headed there, stopping at a gas station along the way to fill the tank.

"Hey, you're Taft's son, aren't you?" said the attendant, a man in his sixties with gray stubble creeping in and out of the folds of his chin. He had a big brown mole that seemed to move inches in any given direction.

"That's right," said Michael. "How'd you know?"

"Recognized the car," answered the man. He rested one arthritic knuckle on the hood. "Yep."

"Oh," said Michael.

"Yep, he talked about you all the time."

Michael froze, not knowing what to say.

"You're that professor, aren't you?"

"Yes," said Michael, a tear threatening to break his stony face wide open like a chisel being brought to bear upon a block of granite with a ten-pound hammer.

"Mighty proud of you he was."

Michael jumped behind the wheel and drove off. The attendant looked at the twenty-dollar bill Michael had given him for seven dollars' worth of regular gasoline.

Mighty proud of you he was. The words echoed through Michael's mind like sounds from a seashell. No matter how fast he drove, he couldn't outrun them. Soon he stopped trying. Michael turned the car around and headed back to town, to the hardware store.

Wordlessly, Michael stalked the aisles searching for Christmas lights, tinsel. He bought a twenty-foot ladder and fifteen gallons of pale green latex paint and six gallons of olive green for the trim. Michael also bought three gallons of pearl-white interior paint. He tossed in a package holding an assortment of six individual brushes in widths varying from one-half an inch to over four inches. He bought a roller and an extension handle.

Michael packed everything in the trunk except the ladder. No matter what he did it or how he fiddled with it, it would stick out. Dangerously. Finally he rolled down all the windows and stuck the ladder in one side and out the other. It wasn't so bad. He kept one hand on the ladder as he drove.

Back at the house, Michael wrestled the ladder out of the car and over to the side wall. It was aluminum but heavier than it looked. He set all the paint supplies on the porch.

He carried the Christmas tree in through the front door, set it plunk down in the middle of the room, then reconsidered and took it back outside.

Michael decided he'd better paint the inside walls first. The tree would only be in the way. Out on the porch, he jimmied open a can of white paint with a small screwdriver and poured some into the roller tray. A bit of color caught his eye. It was a bit of blue and green flashing out of the tiny window of the mailbox beside the door. Michael lifted the wrought iron lid and removed the item. There was only one piece of mail in the box.

A postcard.

Michael held it in the tips of his fingers like a rare stamp. On the cover was a picture of a palm tree swaying in the breeze, off to one side was a fishing pier and, on the beach, a couple danced.

Michael turned the picture postcard over and read the words on the back. It was addressed to Michael. *Merry Christmas*, it said. That was all. It was from Rebecca Greenleaf, his secretary.

Michael took the postcard inside and set it on the shelf in the living room. He moved the postcard only once to paint the wall behind where it stood.

The photograph on Rebecca's postcard confused him, uprooted him. When Michael looked at the pier, he felt the wind blowing against his back. When Michael looked at the couple on the beach, he felt his feet grow warm as if he were dancing on sun-scorched sand. A melody he'd never heard seemed to roam through his mind and through his thoughts like a river of Massachusetts mayflowers with heart-shaped leaves and clusters of small white flowers.

Michael finished painting the living room and put everything in order. He readmitted the Christmas tree and set it up on the stand he'd bought for the occasion. He'd even bought one of those fancy, frilly Christmas tree aprons to go around the tree's base. It was red with white trim, like Santa Claus flattened into a circular stain by a steamroller or one of those car wrecking balls.

The outside of the house took longer. Michael didn't finish until Christmas Eve. His knees were stiff and his hands cracked and bleeding. But his work was done. He'd managed to paint the exterior walls and trim and had made the living room bearable as well. Something had caught at his mind. An idea. Another burr. He found a tiny, half-rusted can of bright yellow enamel on a metal shelf in the garage. With a small, pointed brush, he painted two sunflowers, one on each side of the mailbox.

He didn't even know why he did it.

His mother and father's room was beyond his immediate means. He'd tacked up an extra blanket where their door should have been. It would do for the time being.

The time being what it was.

Michael took the longest, hottest shower of his life, rinsing and scraping paint splotches from his sunburned skin with towel and fingernail.

He shaved and brushed his teeth for the first time in days.

Michael hadn't thought to wash any clothes and his father's things wouldn't have fit him even if he could have borne the thought of wearing them. He was forced to put on the same clothes he'd been painting in for the last two days. He found a can of baby powder in the bathroom and sprinkled his pants and shirt liberally.

It couldn't hurt.

Before he departed, Michael turned on the Christmas lights, the ones he'd strung up on the house and the ones he'd hung inside the living room window. He left the Oldsmobile in the driveway. After all, Ellen and Alex lived up the street. He didn't need a car.

Michael stood at the sidewalk and looked back at the house with pride. It was the first time in his adult life that he'd done anything like it. Decorations, a Christmas tree. Celebrations. Still, why be alone? Why should he be alone? Why should Ellen and Alex be alone when they cared for one another?

Michael traversed the sidewalk with satisfaction and mounting excitement. It was Christmas Eve and he felt beneficent.

A row of big bright Christmas lights surrounded Ellen's

front window. A solitary plastic baby reindeer in the yard, head bent, pretended to nibble the tough Florida grass. Michael's generally dour expression broke into a grin.

He knocked. Ellen answered.

"Michael," she exclaimed, more than modestly stunned.

"Hi."

"Hi. I-how are you?"

"Good," replied Michael. Ellen watched him, one hand on the doorknob and one on the door frame, blocking his entrance. Michael waited for Ellen to pick up the conversation. He'd already used up his somewhat vacant social skills and vocabulary.

Ellen said, "It's good to see you. I'm glad you're feeling better, Michael."

"Yes, much better. Look, I—" stumbled Michael. "I painted the house and fixed up the Christmas lights and bought a tree and all and, you see, I was wondering if you and Alex would like to come over for Christmas Eve? No point in spending it all alone." Had all those words spilled out of his mouth? Ellen seemed as surprised as Michael himself.

Ellen's eyes changed color but Michael didn't notice. "Oh, Michael," she said. "That's really very nice of you, but," she looked back into the living room, "I'm afraid I already have a guest."

Michael shifted to one side and casually peeked in the opening between Ellen and door. A personable young man, drink in hand (in a Christmas decorated mug—basically Santa Claus with the top of his skull removed—who says holidays aren't festive any longer?) sat on the sofa. He wore dark dress pants and a sports coat. A wide hideously green tie hung from his neck. His red hair a stark crew cut. In honor of Christmas, Michael supposed.

Michael took a step back. "I'm sorry," he stuttered. "I didn't realize."

"No, it's all right." Ellen excused herself. "Could you wait here a moment?"

Michael nodded and Ellen went back to the living room, closing the front door discreetly behind her. Michael stared at the Pasternak nameplate beside the door, feeling every bit the idiot.

In a minute she returned, with her son, Alex, in tow.

"Listen, Michael," she said, "Why don't you come inside and join us? We're just listening to Christmas music and talking. It'll be fun. Won't it, Alex, dear?"

"Yeah," said Alex. "You should. I'm going to open my presents tomorrow but you can look at the packages and help me guess what they are. I bet you never guess what I got Mom."

"Thank you, anyway, but I shouldn't. I only wanted to wish you both Merry Christmas."

"Thanks," said Alex. "Merry Christmas to you, too."

"Ellen," said Michael, "could I speak to you alone for a moment?"

Ellen nodded and sent Alex on his way. "I'll be in in a minute, dear."

"Listen, Michael—" started Ellen.

"No." He thrust his arms up as if to parry her words. "You don't have to say anything. I don't know what I was thinking. I had no business coming over here on Christmas Eve of all days and forcing myself on the two of you." He glanced at the house. "You have your own lives to lead."

Ellen sighed and explained. "His name is Louis. He works at the same school that I do. He's always been nice to me. So I invited him over here. He doesn't have any family in town and it's Christmas and—"

And Michael hadn't even bothered to telephone or show any interest in her. He'd never even asked her what she was doing for Christmas. Ellen liked Michael. She'd liked him a lot. But he'd constantly pushed her away. She didn't know if Louis was the right man for her, no one was with her husband gone. But she had to try. And having met Michael, having spent time with him, opened something up inside her, something that wanted to stick its head up out of the sand and at least see what it was missing and if there was anything there it wanted or needed.

Michael hadn't wanted her. And, since the fire, he had ignored her wholly.

"You could come in—" she offered again.

"No, I'd better leave." Michael retreated.

"Goodbye then, Michael," she said. "Merry Christmas."

"Merry Christmas," repeated Michael, his feet kicking up imagined clods of snow as he trudged down the sidewalk through imaginary drifts that blocked his imagined way.

# 52

Michael didn't remember packing.

Besides the grocery bag stuffed with dirty underwear, dirty socks, dirty shoes and dirty trousers and shirts, Michael found himself hauling one ancient concertina and one equally ancient cribbage board. The concertina had survived the fire. The cribbage board had survived the century and the humidity of the years spent in a Florida attic. He also carried off a cardboard box full of old family photos. A shoebox. Ladies heels, size seven. Todesco was the brand name. Imported from Italy. The box was a shade of purple. Hadn't he read a story somewhere about the universe running out of purple?

Before embarking, Michael plugged in the Christmas tree lights. The colored lights blinked steadily, giving life to the otherwise lifeless room. He took the postcard from Rebecca off the shelf. He didn't know why. He stuck it in the crumpled grocery sack with the rest of his belongings. Michael pulled open the curtains so all Taft and Marie's neighbors would see the blinking Christmas tree. He left on the outside Christmas lights as well.

The lights shone long after Michael had abandoned the house and fled in Taft's Oldsmobile. That Oldsmobile was working overtime.

Halfway to Michigan, Michael turned left.

He'd made it as far as Lexington, Kentucky. That was something. He passed fertile Kentucky blue grass and herds of racehorses and fields of tobacco. Thoroughbreds, mentholated cigarette butts dangling from their mouths, seemed to grin at him from between fresh-painted white stockade fences as he passed them.

The next thing Michael knew, he was heading west towards St. Louis. Michael stopped at a motel with a big orange sign dangling over the freeway and took a room. He met a girl who was sitting on the second-floor steps and crying. She was young enough to be a college student. She had a southern accent and a clear complexion. Wearing dirty blue slacks and a beige sweater of some synthetic fiber, she was crying. Her boyfriend had abandoned her there, she'd said.

Michael invited her to his room. He'd intended to share only his bed with her, not his body. But then she'd asked him, point blank, to make love to her.

"Aren't you going to make love to me?" she'd whispered almost mournfully as they lay under the covers side by side and so he tried.

But he felt nothing and gave up.

Without saying a word, Michael rose, taking only the top cover with him and slept on the hard floor.

"What's wrong?" she'd whispered from the bed.

"Nothing. I'm sorry," he said. He heard her crying again. But there was nothing he could do. In the morning, Michael gave the girl a ride to a friend's house in town and said goodbye. He still didn't know her name so he only said "Goodbye." Not "Goodbye, Sally," or "Goodbye, Sue." Just goodbye.

Michael made his way back to the freeway and headed west again. The city of St. Louis turned its back on him.

Kansas City, both of them, came on fast. Home of one of the largest livestock exchange buildings in the world. Rebecca would cringe to go near it. The smell of blood and echo of frightened herd animals hovered ghostlike, a cloud of violence threatening to rain down on the city.

Physically drained, Michael stopped early. He took a motel room and had a pizza delivered to him. He paid the delivery boy and gave him a dollar tip. Christmas had come and gone. Why be extravagant?

Michael didn't know what day it was. He set his keys on top the television bolted to the bureau. He'd been so used to using televisions as tables that he didn't think to turn the set on.

Besides, there wasn't any news that he wanted to hear.

Michael left the following morning taking cold pizza, barely insulated in thin greasy cardboard, with him. It was freezing outside and he had no warm clothes. He turned the car heater on full blast and it blew in his face like radioactive wind.

Stark wheat fields hosting shivering cattle marked the road. He swore they were the same cows he'd seen in Florida weeks ago. Only these cows seemed to be staring at him. As if he were crazy. Steam poured out their nostrils as if by magic, or as if they were dragons hiding in lumpy cow bodies, hiding in these awkward conditions until mankind chose to believe in dragons once again. Then they would shed their cowhides and spread their dragon wings anew, flying over fields of fresh mown wheat and chasing down fair damsels...

It was a future worth waiting for, if you were a dragon.

Unbeknownst to Michael, Einstein followed in the car behind. Stalking him. The driver of the Ford pickup tailing him was a book collector on his way to Denver. Crates of books for trade filled the flatbed. One especially valuable book in the driver's possession was an autographed biography of Albert Einstein written by a friend and colleague of the man's.

This book the man kept in a leather case inside the cab on the seat beside him. It was too valuable to be kept with the others. The other book he kept in that case was 'L'onanisme, ou dissertation sur les maladies produites par la masturbation,' by Tissot. The 1760 edition. Alexandre Dumas once possessed this very copy himself. He'd won it in a fight with a school mate named Bligny from Villers-Cotterets.

These days Alexandre (pere) preferred Kurt Vonnegut and even westerns such as those by Louis L'Amour. Though he still kept his eye open for good French erotica. There was no substitute for this. Even in the Afterlife.

In Denver, the book dealer turned off near Aurora. Michael turned off here, too. The men each checked into rooms at one of several chain motels across from the mall. The rooms were adjoining with a locked door between them. If the photodimension had had legs Einstein could have crept through the slit between the bottom of the door and carpet and into Michael's room. He could have seen Michael lying in bed, sleepless, restless. A lost soul.

Taft came to him when he managed to dream at all. Michael pictured his father as a young man, Michael's age. He could no longer imagine him being old. Try as he might, he could only see his father as a young man, not an old one. Not a dead one.

In one recurring dream, Michael was at Sanchi, in India, excavating a tope—an artificial mound, a solid cone of masonry surrounded by a low circular wall, built to house relics of the Buddha (the Buddha seemed to leave a lot of relics lying around —he was not, apparently, the fastidious type).

Michael, trowel taped like a mummy's bandage to his hand, dug round the perimeter. The tope at Sanchi is about 42 feet high and 106 feet in diameter. Michael dug. When he reached the bottom, Michael came to a clear plexiglass shell. Inside was his father, sitting in his recliner, reading The Three Musketeers. Alexandre Dumas slouched on the sofa, playing with his son, Al Jr. Their dog rested his head on the hearth and cracked open cherry pits with his heavy jaws.

It was the Guggenheim Museum, empty but for three men and a dog sorely in need of bathing.

Sometimes Taft would chuckle and Alexandre Dumas would raise his head and say "What? What? What is it?" Wanting to know what Taft thought of his book, and if he was laughing in all the right parts. Usually he was.

Taft was confused. He remembered dying, or what he took to be death. He could hear Marie screaming. She was yelling at him. Telling him not to do it. But he did it anyway. The next thing he knew she was yelling at Michael about something. It sounded something like fire, or don't burn down the house or don't burn the toast.

It made no sense to Taft and so he'd turned his attention

elsewhere.

And then she painted herself away. When he'd turned backwards to see what he'd left behind, he found himself walking or being sucked into another painting (as if a god-sized lamprey had sucked him from one universe to another) facing a scene that looked exactly like that painting by Grant Wood called Midnight Ride of Paul Revere.

Paul and his horse galumphed by, both rider and horse bellowing "Taft Hart is coming! Taft Hart is coming!" Taft didn't know which surprised him more, hearing Paul Revere, who was two hundred years dead, announce his coming, or hearing that talking horse.

Funny thing was, the horse sounded more human than Paul had. Paul had a high, squeaky, girlish voice. Not the kind of voice at all that Taft, as a child, had imagined riding through the dangerous Massachusetts countryside warning his countrymen about the invading English devils.

The horse's voice, in contrast, was deep and masculine.

# 53

The dealer in rare books' name was Salmo Clarki. Einstein stayed with him through that book convention. There were no bids sufficiently satisfying to Salmo that he would be able to part with this edition easily. And so he kept it. He had bought the book for an investment and now he had grown quite fond of having it around. From show to show, from town to town, Einstein and Dumas kept him company. In their own way, they too, were three musketeers.

For Salmo knew about the photodimension also. Not that he understood it or could draw you a diagram of it, not even if you'd begged him but, in his bones, he knew it was there. He knew that Einstein watched him. He knew that Alexandre Dumas was watching too, and writing...

Sometimes, when the night was warm and the wine copious, Alexandre told his stories. Reminiscences of the days of his youth. Perhaps a tale about the thin, dark and lovely Melanie Waldor, who fanned his emotions in 1827. He still kept the corsage of geraniums that Melanie had removed from over her breast at a warm September's ball. At the end of the waltz, with Alexandre, she had gifted him those lucky flowers. Alexandre put his lips to those petals as if they were her body and soul.

O, how he'd loved her then. Perhaps it was that she was married and a mother that made him want her all the more madly.

Alexandre had a way with words. That was certain.

Al, Al and Sal. They traveled by pickup truck.

# 54

Michael slid side-to-side across the highway.

Ice everywhere. Not that he minded. All the danger gave him something to occupy his mind. Whenever a big semi came rolling by, he hugged the side of the road. They flew over the ice as if it were a racetrack, not hesitating at all.

Michael spent two days and nights fighting the cold and ice in a town called Moab in Utah, near Arches National Park, an area known for its fantastic natural sandstone formations, like the Landscape Arch and the Eye of the Whale.

There, Michael met a girl with fuzzy, strawberry blonde hair and a body, under all that thermal wrapping, like a Titian nude. She had more soft flesh than firm and four hundred and fifty years ago she'd have been a Renaissance beauty. A real looker.

She went by the name Joan and said she taught elementary school in Provo. She was single, thirty-five years old and four years divorced. Once, Michael saw her smoke a cigarette and her lips barely moved. Michael bought her drinks and she put her hand on his thigh. He spent his second night beneath the covers in her room, abandoning his own to the cold.

Michael had sex with her and did all the things she asked. She asked him what he liked and he said it didn't matter. Once, he closed his eyes and imagined he was having sex with Ellen, pulling off her bathing suit and making love underneath the picnic table at some unspecified beach in Florida.

In the morning, Michael rose and returned to his own freezing room. The heat had been off all night. It was five in the morning and dark as hell. He put his things back in his paper sack and tossed the sack in the car. He'd have taken a shower but it was too cold even for a hot shower.

Michael glanced at her room (the blackout curtains pulled tight) as he started the car. What Joan wanted most of all in life was to be happy. Though she slept, unaware of the world's reality around her, unaware of Michael's being gone, her sleep was a sad one. Her shallow breaths, sad breaths. Her heart beats hollow and unfulfilled. She had wanted to fall in love, but hadn't.

Michael took one fleeting look as he gingerly pulled out of the nearly snowbound parking lot. The curtains didn't move.

He did.

# 55

Michael thought about his sisters back in Michigan. They'd probably all been together at Christmas. Sisters, brothers-in-law, nieces, cousins, the whole lot of them. Had they enjoyed it? Could they enjoy it with their mother and father so soon dead? They'd probably had a big Christmas tree and gotten together at Cora's house. After all, her place was the biggest. New Year's ditto.

Michael thought, too, about Ellen and her son, Alex. What were they doing? Did they have a nice Christmas? There were moments when he was tempted to turn the car around and drive straight to their house and check. To ask them, "Did you have a nice Christmas?" To see the gifts that Ellen most probably bestowed generously on her only son, and to see the gift that Alex had given to his mother. To see if the Christmas lights still shone at Taft and Marie's house.

But Michael never turned the car around. He couldn't. He just couldn't. He couldn't turn the car around. Not even the length of a parking lot. He couldn't turn the car around. If he did...

If he did, all would be lost. He would be lost. He'd be sucked up into another dimension or lost inside himself.

Onward he went.

Utah transmogrified into Nevada and he followed Route 50. He spent one night in Ely and another in Carson City lodged in a squat gray motor lodge in the vicinity of the Nevada State Prison. Michael lay in bed and imagined atomic weapons tests being conducted in deep hollow tunnels beneath him; their radioactive particles sweeping upward into his system. One day, maybe he too would contract cancer and maybe it would all be because he'd spent the night in a not too clean Nevada motel room with flaking paint and soiled carpets, a leaky toilet and nuclear explosions going on beneath him.

Michael rose, fetched the down jacket he'd bought in Moab from the chair where it had fallen, put it on, zipped it up and climbed back into bed. Maybe all those goose feathers would protect him from the neutrons, positrons and deadlier-than-thou-trons out to get him.

He slept fitfully.

In the morning, Michael ate in the diner across the road from the motel. The only restaurant in sight. The sign said JOE'S but Joe had gotten smart and sold out years ago. The landscape was snow- and mud-colored. Michael sat at the counter beside two men, one middle aged and one in his twenties, whom he soon discovered to be prison guards. They amused Michael with their tales of bungled prison breaks and even more extreme tales about the lengths to which some prisoners would go to satisfy their stymied sexual urges.

Michael drank coffee, two gulps per cup, and ate one egg, well-done.

He put four one-dollar bills on the counter (which included a generous tip) and he left. He hiked across the street to the car which he'd already packed.

Suddenly he was in California.

# 56

School stood in recess, the campus nearly deserted.

Here, along the dark Pacific Ocean, the wind blew coldly. Fog spread over the coast and was slow to retreat. Michael walked to the anthropology building with a deep sense of unease.

He had an appointment with the chairman of the department, Randall Cane, a handsome man in his own way and affable if not crossed. This was not a meeting he was looking forward to convening.

The maintenance crew had freshly waxed the tile floor. Barely a scuff mark remained. The custodians went ferociously about their business with the students out of town. He took the shining steps and crossed the hallway.

Classes would be starting up again soon and then the custodian's job would simply be to maintain. That was the best that Michael could hope for as well, to maintain. And he feared even his ability to do that any longer.

Randall Cane waited in his office, behind his well-appointed desk. Rebecca, was nowhere to be seen.

"Michael!" Randall rose from his green leather chair and shook Michael's hand effusively. Michael shook it back. In his own way, Randall had always been a friend.

Randall sat and Michael followed the procedure.

"First," said Randall, a look of proper concern and melancholy on his visage, "I am sorry." Randall didn't know exactly what words to use. He'd never known anyone who'd lost his mother and father so quickly in succession.

Michael stared past Randall at the walnut bookcases towering behind. All those books seemed like different worlds, different realities, blue spines, red, yellow, black, magenta. He had only to pluck one from the shelf and he might be transported to any one of an infinite number of worlds, existences. Which book would he choose, Michael wondered? Or should he tempt fate and close his eyes and let his hands alone decide?

"Michael?"

Michael jerked open his eyes.

"Are you all right?" asked Randall. He leaned forward over his desk, his thin hands splayed like chicken's feet across the blotter.

"Yes. I guess I'm a little tired yet."

Randall nodded. Michael had telephoned him the evening past and explained that he'd only just arrived by car from Florida. That was the first surprise. Michael called for this meeting, begged for it, in fact. As a friend and a colleague, Randall couldn't refuse. He was shocked by Michael's appearance —scruffy, paint spattered clothing and a scraggly beard. That was the second surprise.

Michael handed Randall a legal-sized manilla envelope. "What's this," said Randall, turning the unmarked envelope over in his hand.

"Open it," Michael said. "It's my resignation." He'd scribbled it down on motel stationary somewhere in north-central California.

Randall glowered and tore open the envelope with a whale bone letter opener carved by the adept hands of a Haida craftsmen. The Haida Indians of British Columbia are skillful carvers. Though originally a ceremonial knife, the bone served Randall well as a letter disemboweler. The nether end displayed the totem of the man who'd carved it. A rendition of a bear.

Randall Cane read the hastily crafted and written letter of resignation dutifully. "Well, well." He took the letter and the envelope belonging to it and set it in the trash can beneath his desk. "I'll file this."

Michael tried to follow the man's hand under the table but

his view was blocked off in front by the panel along the back of the desk. "What did you do with it?" He hadn't seen the chairman open any drawers.

Randall scribbled on paper of his own now. Michael started to speak but Randall put him off with a lift of the hand. "Here," he said, handing Michael a hastily improvised document of his own devising.

Michael took the letter warily and read it over quickly. His eyebrows twitched and his mouth quivered. "What's this?"

"I'm afraid I can't accept your resignation, Michael. And if pushed," he threatened half-jokingly, "I'll have you committed for psychiatric observation. That is my granting you a leave of absence, with pay for the next full semester. That means I expect you back for summer sessions and I expect you to complete your manuscript on the Mexico work you've been up to."

"But I quit!" insisted Michael.

"You're a tenured professor, Michael. Don't throw it away. Take some time to get over your grief. Do some work, take a vacation. It'll do you good to get away from the classroom end of things for a while."

Randall rose and escorted Michael to the door. The secretary's desk stood empty. "Besides," he quipped, "you work for the state, you can't quit. Take a close look at your contract. One day the state will even bury you in a state provided grave in a state provided cemetery for retired-expired archaeologists."

Randall was all smiles. "In a hundred years, young archaeology graduate students will be coming along digging up your bones and studying you in return. It's all in the fine print."

"But—"

"Off you go now." Randall pushed Michael out the door.

Rebecca ran into Michael in the hallway. "Hi, Michael!" she exclaimed, a look of unexpected joy on her face.

Michael didn't see her happy mien. He only barely acknowledged her fleshly presence. "Hi," he said in passing, hands stuffed in his pockets. He didn't stop or even slow down all the way home.

Elizabeth telephoned and he refused to speak with her. Cora called. "Leave me alone," he said and hung up. Mary didn't even try. Mary put flowers on her mother and father's graves and prayed for everyone, her brother included.

Michael paced in his condo like a primate slowly going mad at the LA Zoo. Just what the hell was he supposed to do for the next six months? Warren Zevon pounded on the door, banged away at his temples, demanded to see the desperado inside. What the hell was he supposed to do?

He stood in front of the bathroom mirror nervously biting the inside of his cheeks. He ate all his food cold out of cans or room temperature from plastic bags he ripped open with his teeth. He was going mad. As if he hadn't already been there and back. Twice.

The first day of classes, he returned to campus, went to his office, and pretended to work.

"What are you doing here?" demanded Paul Bandry, the social anthropologist, poking his nose in, wearing a Mexican style guaybara shirt and dress slacks with espadrilles and black stockings.

Paul was a gingerbread sort of figure with sun-hewn skin and hair that stuck up an inch over his head no matter how much he tried to flatten it down with every oily concoction known to man. A Salvadoran woman had once massaged a dose of dung beetle juice in his hair. While it had managed to hold his hair down, it gave him an unbearable pink rash. His girth was nearly as great as his height. He had small hands and tiny fingers, like little Vienna sausages. It was a wonder to watch him work his computer keyboard, let alone anything more complicated, like an old school reel-to-reel film projector.

"Working," said Michael, barely sociable himself.

"I thought you were on a leave of absence."

"It's a working vacation," Michael answered testily.

"I see." Paul prattled on, bravely attempting conversation, "How was Florida? How's your mom doing?" He fired off the questions in rapid, stupid fashion. Professor Bandry had been in Guatemala and only returned over the weekend. No one had filled him in on Michael's predicament and tribulations. He'd only known that Michael was supposed to be on an extended leave.

Michael rose. His chair shot against the wall behind with a report like a sledge hammer falling on an empty metal file cabinet. "She's dead!" he shouted, his face glowing purple. "She's dead. He's dead." He waved his arms. "THEY'RE ALL DEAD!" Michael stepped menacingly towards the social anthropologist who'd faced many tribes in his career but never been nearly so scared in all his life.

Michael was in his face. Paul could feel Michael's breath as he raged. "Everybody's dead. Didn't you know? Haven't you heard?"

Rebecca ran into the office, Randall Cane right behind her.

Paul Bandry stood there, his back against the door, blustering. "I'm sorry," he said, truly anguished, not to mention mortally frightened. "I didn't know," he said to Rebecca and Randall. "Who's dead?"

"I'm an archaeologist!" hollered Michael. "They're all dead! I STUDY THE DEAD!"

"Michael!" barked Randall. Michael froze, arms akimbo. "I'd like a word with you."

Professor Bandry looked appealingly at Michael. "I'm sorry, Michael."

"Come on, Professor Bandry," said Rebecca, "I'll get you some tea." She took the shaken professor by the arm and led him to the tiny lunchroom the department kept around the corner from her office. The room contained an old conference table and several worn out chairs. Rebecca dutifully maintained hot water on tap for tea and a fresh pot of coffee every two hours.

Hardly anyone used the tiny yellow refrigerator in the corner, not for its intended use, that is. She was forever finding dung samples wrapped in plastic bags inside the refrigerator. The physical anthropologist liked to store them there, no matter how much and how often she'd exhorted him not to.

Randall closed the door to Michael's office.

Michael clutched his aching head and tried to pull his face apart, in several directions at once, like a lump of Silly Putty.

"Sorry," he said, a truthful ring of atonement in his overly tired voice.

Randall sighed. "I know." Neither man spoke as the clock rounded off another minute. "Michael, I think you should work at home. Better yet, take a vacation."

"I'm not good at vacations. Besides, I've just had one, remember?" Bitterness soaked through his words.

"I mean a real one."

Michael shook his head no.

"Fine but I don't want to see you on campus for a while. Nothing personal." Randall rose and opened the door. Before Randall went out, he added, "There's nothing anyone can do for you if you're not willing to let them in."

Michael sat at his desk unmoving, no longer pretending to work, no longer pretending that he might.

# 57

Though he couldn't remember the name and he didn't quite remember the street, with a little luck Michael found the Golden Apple restaurant, the little place Rebecca had taken him to. When was that? Two? Three lifetimes ago?

He ordered a tofu shake and a tofu burger. It was the same meal he'd ordered his first time there. Michael was brave enough to come back a second time but not brave enough to try one of the other more exotic sounding items on the menu, such as the eggplant spaghetti or the zucchini pita pizza.

Michael ate at a small table beneath a photograph of Albert Einstein. Funny, he didn't remember seeing that picture there before, though, of course, it had been there all along. Someone, the proprietor, had cleaned the glass protecting it with ammonia and water and moved it front and center. Albert's gaze was now clear and unblurred, though the ammonia had brought tears of irritation to his eyes at the time. (Couldn't the proprietor have only used a damp cloth?) Albert knew Michael well. He was Taft and Marie's boy, after all.

They spoke of him often.

Though the Golden Apple was very nearly deserted, Michael couldn't escape the feeling he was being watched. He ate his sandwich quickly and departed.

Lately, since his mother and father passed on, Michael had been having the oddest sensations. Sometimes, at all the strangest times and in all the strangest places, he'd hear accordion music. And voices.

Not voices telling him things. They told him nothing. Just voices talking. As if he were hearing the voices of people long dead. Their voices echoed over the earth, like memories, refusing to die or fade away.

Michael's grandfather called him. His mother called him. Katrina, Great Grandmother of All Trout even whispered his name. Incredibly enough, it was his father who called to him the loudest. . .

Back home, Michael took out the concertina and looked at it. He ran his fingers over the keys. The cribbage board lay on the coffee table in the living room, waiting for players to take their chances. So was the shoebox full of photographs. Michael shuffled through them. Odd, there was an old black and white snapshot of Albert Einstein among the bunch. What was that doing there?

# 58

Michael called his boss, Randall Cane. "I know you don't want to see me—at the university, that is," said Michael from the telephone in his kitchen. Rebecca's postcard of the young couple dancing on the beach beside the pier jumped into view. Funny, he didn't remember taping it to the refrigerator. "But I hope you don't mind my calling."

"It's okay." said Randall, on the other end of the line which was attached to his office. "What can I do for you?"

"I'm planning a trip and I wanted to collect a few things before I leave. I'll be back for summer, I promise," said Michael. "And I won't yell at anyone while I'm up there."

"Of course, Michael," Randall agreed unequivocally.

Michael went to the office the next morning around ten o'clock. Paul Bandry had stayed politely away. Michael sought him out. He went to Paul's office and found him hunched over his desk. Michael apologized for his earlier untoward and certainly uncalled for behavior.

Paul said to forget it. "Perfectly understandable," he'd said, perfectly understanding.

Michael gathered up the few notes he thought he might need from his files. He said so long to Randall and left a note for the secretary, who never seemed to be at her desk, leaving instructions on the disposition of his mail while he was to be away. Why was the woman never at her desk?

Outside, beyond the protection of the dark walls of the Anthropology Building the sun twisted brightly down. Michael sneezed. A reaction to the light.

He turned and took a last look at the college. Oh, Michael knew he'd be back. Only he also knew, he had a feeling, that things wouldn't look the same when he got back. For the first time in his life, Michael didn't know where he was going and found that it didn't matter. He'd walked to his car on automatic and hadn't noticed that there was someone standing beside it.

He came to a startled halt. "Rebecca—"

"Hi." When she spoke, her voice came out subdued and nervous, yet full of unspoken intent. Her hair fell loose in the still air. She was wearing a bright tie-dye dress (splashes of purple and red and yellow) and comfortable Birkenstock sandals.

"How are you?"

Rebecca nearly fell over. Michael asking someone how they were?

"I'm fine," she replied. "And you?"

Michael shrugged. It was the most exercise his shoulders got these days. "Okay, I suppose."

"That's good," she answered. She wasn't as sure of herself as she'd hoped to be.

"Well," muttered Michael apologetically, "I have to be going."

"I know," said Rebecca. "I'm going with you."

It was then that the object dangling from Rebecca's arm registered in Michael's somewhat bruised brain. A blue suitcase.

"What do you mean?" he asked stupidly. "Can I give you a lift somewhere?"

"Where are you going?"

"I don't know," he answered honestly.

Rebecca nodded knowingly. "That's okay," she said. "I'll go with you. Open the door so I can put this in." The suitcase was rather heavy for its size. She hadn't wanted to appear overbearing so she'd crammed as much as she could into the one small bag. After all, she didn't want to scare Michael off, did she?

Her arm was numb from shoulder to fingers and threatened to pull loose from its socket from holding onto the thing in the parking lot. Rebecca had refused to let it rest on the ground, the suitcase had to stay in her hands, safely in her grip, until this moment was over.

Michael stared dumbly.

"Well?"

"Right." Michael unlocked the car door and Rebecca, shooting him a grin, tossed her suitcase onto the backseat.

"I'll take those," she said, taking Michael's papers from his hands and setting them on the floor in back. "They'll be okay there. Hop in."

Michael started obediently for the door then stopped in the vicinity of the trunk. "Wait a minute" he said, echoes of Marie's voice, kicking up like dust in his path, "I don't even know where I'm going. I might be gone for months. You can't just barge in and join me."

She looked at him, patiently smiling.

"Besides, your job—"

"I've got leave as well."

"Randall Cane gave you a leave of absence?" he said in disbelief.

"Well, not exactly," she confessed. "I had to quit. But Professor Cane said that he'd hold my job open for me for as long as he could. He said it could take months to find a suitable replacement. He's already got a temp from personnel. He's such a sweet man."

Rebecca reached over and unlocked Michael's door. "Come on."

Michael shut his eyes and tilted his head to the sun, still twisting overhead. The sun shot photons at him with keen accuracy, as if each pore of his skin was a tiny, highly specialized photon receptor. Michael didn't mind. He had bigger fish to fry. Not that you couldn't have fried one hell of a fish on the surface of the sun. Each photon seemed to rain on him like a dream. A tiny molecular memory worming its way into his mind.

Michael found himself behind the wheel. Rebecca placed her hands in her lap. He could have fought with her. He could have argued with her. He could have ordered her out of the car. Not that he thought it would do any good.

Michael had seen her type before. They never took no for an answer. They were crazy alright.

"So," said Rebecca lightly, mustering her courage because this was life and there was no point in doing it halfway. Rebecca settled back into her seat and clipped on her seatbelt. She looked straight ahead. "Where are we going?"

Michael rolled down the window. Alexandre Dumas died on the evening of December the fifth in the year 1870. Alexandre Dumas (fils), because of the exigencies and inconveniences of war (the Prussians could be so unreasonable) and personal considerations, was not able to bury his father properly and permanently until April the 16th in 1872 when he removed his father's body from its temporary resting place in the cemetery of the small church in Neuville-les-Pollet and returned his father's remains to Villers-Cotterets and prayed for his father's soul in a grave alongside the general, his father's father and Marie-Louise Labouret, his equally loved father's mother.

So.

Sometimes sons can be a bit late. Often through no fault of their own. The world goes on with or without us. Streams converge and diverge. Einstein plays cribbage in the photodimension, oblivious to it all.

Michael turned and aimed the car at Michigan. "I never said goodbye to my father."

# ABOUT THE AUTHOR

## Glenn Eric

Glenn Eric is a bestselling and critically acclaimed author writing under multiple names, in addition to being a successful singer-songwriter. For more about the author, please check out social media and visit GlennEric.com.

# BOOKS BY THIS AUTHOR

## Bad Vibrations

Sometimes a house is NOT a home. Bad Vibrations tells the story of a man coming apart at the seams. When a mid-list romance author moves with his wife from NYC to the Blue Ridge Mountains of NC for a change of scenery, little does he know that his life is about to take a hard turn into the Twilight Zone.

## After The Fall

Jeff Talbot was an artist. And a husband and a father. He thought he had everything he wanted—and he did. Until the day his second child, a daughter, Christy, was born. His wife, Emily, went into a coma that day and never recovered. He had to raise his son and new daughter alone. He moved to a farm, away from the crowds and tried his best. But his relationship with his oldest child, Ben, grew strained. The day that Christy fell down the stairs to her death was the day that something in Jeff Talbot died, too, on the inside. And it's going to take a long time and a lot of searching before he finds what's missing. Filled with magic realism, After The Fall is the story of a man haunted by the death of his daughter, a man whose pain and suffering lead him to the brink of insanity. And it might take a crazy bird to lead him back…

## A Life Untold

Orville and Wilbur Wright came to the North Carolina coast for the strong, steady winds. Daniel Cross has come for something almost as intangible. He comes seeking a new place that he and Noah can call home. Someplace with a future and not a past. Uprooting the two of them from Boston had been a sudden decision—based on nothing more than Daniel's perception that Noah was growing more withdrawn and he blamed that on Boston. Perhaps that decision had been a rash one. Now, he is determined to make the best of it.

Samantha Rivers works with her father at Rivers Motorcycle Sales & Service. Is she happy? Maybe not, but she is satisfied and wants only for things to stay the same. When Daniel Cross shows up and buys a junk motorcycle, she thinks he's crazy. And annoying. The feeling is mutual. But then something changes and the small act of buying and rebuilding a motorcycle becomes the catalyst that draws them closer while tearing them apart and putting them back together again too.

A reflection on love and life for fans of Nicholas Sparks and Jojo Moyes.

## To The Stars Forever

An old-fashioned adventure of the future... It's a not-so-brave new world. Corporations rule humanity. The world is a bleak and unkind place. But then the Mitoc, powerful aliens from the distant reaches of the universe, came and things got worse. Humans found themselves unable to resist the Mitoc's call. Like sheep, they climbed aboard the vast alien spaceships, to be shipped off to the stars to fight the alien race's war for them. To die for them.

Because millions of years ago, the Mitoc seeded Earth and a million other worlds. Programming the human species' genetic code so when the time came, humans would have no choice but to obey them. All so that when the time was right and the creatures the Mitoc engineered were advanced enough, they would come scoop them up by the millions to fight and die for them in their timeless battle with their own relentless enemy.

This is the story of one small group of genetic defectives who, although immune to the Mitoc's call, find themselves aboard a Mitoc ship. They are dropped on a planet in a far away galaxy to fight an enemy they never knew existed and a war they care nothing about.

www.ingramcontent.com/pod-product-compliance
Lightning Source LLC
Chambersburg PA
CBHW030519020726
47494CB00004B/1152